OVERNIGHT WIFE

Mollie Molay

Harlequin Books

TORONTO • NEW YORK • LONDON
AMSTERDAM • PARIS • SYDNEY • HAMBURG
STOCKHOLM • ATHENS • TOKYO • MILAN
MADRID • WARSAW • BUDAPEST • AUCKLAND

For Karen Pershing, my first writing instructor,
for putting up with me.

And for Harriet Heaton Ammons, a dear friend who
tells me she always knew I could get here from there.

ISBN 0-373-16703-2

OVERNIGHT WIFE

Copyright © 1997 by Mollie Molé.

Printed in U.S.A.

His dark eyes seemed to see right through her. "That is, if you have a husband."

"I do," Arden answered, hiding her ringless hand in the folds of her wedding gown. "He's...he's out looking for a cab."

He opened his overcoat and tucked the briefcase behind him. "Come on in," he coaxed. "I don't bite."

Luke McCauley appeared to be everything Arden had dreamed about since she'd been old enough to dream. Incredibly sexy, confident, with an air of mystery about him. The exact opposite of everything she'd been taught to want—and exactly what made her pulse pound. Her father's warnings were no match for this man's steady gaze and his open hands that seemed to dare her to take the chance.

In one swift motion Arden tossed her bridal bouquet into the trash can beside her and stepped into his arms. If she was on the road to ruin, she intended to enjoy the ride!

ABOUT THE AUTHOR

For Mollie Molay, writing this story was like reliving a memory. In March of 1993, during one of the biggest storms of the century, Mollie spent a night at New York's Kennedy Airport—and lived to tell the tale! Most of the incidents mentioned here actually took place, including a contingent of Frenchmen leaping over the ticket counter to attack the agents! Though Mollie can still feel the cold floor she spent the night on, she didn't find a man like Luke McCauley.

Books by Mollie Molay

HARLEQUIN AMERICAN ROMANCE
560—FROM DRIFTER TO DADDY
597—HER TWO HUSBANDS
616—MARRIAGE BY MISTAKE
638—LIKE FATHER, LIKE SON
682—NANNY & THE BODYGUARD

Prologue

"Margo," Arden Crandall whispered as the church organist began to play. "I don't think I can go through with this!"

"Sure you can, honey," Margo soothed. "You're just having premarital jitters. I've heard every bride feels this way. All you have to remember is that your John's a great guy. A little older than you, but then..." She paused, winked and grinned.

"Then, what?"

"Now, Arden, you know your father wouldn't like me talking like this. And certainly not in church. But not to worry, I'm sure everything's going to work out fine. You'll see." She handed Arden the bouquet of red and white roses and maidenhair ferns, just perfect for her Christmas Eve wedding.

Margo Cummings, Arden's best friend and maid of honor, made a last-minute adjustment to the head wreath of white winter roses that encircled Arden's nest of blond curls. An attached veil flowed down the bride's back to her waist.

Arden's hands trembled as she took a deep breath

to steady herself. This was supposed to be the happiest day of her life.

Outside the vestry door, she could hear the arrival of last-minute wedding guests. The organist segued into a popular love song. A song she'd insisted upon after her father's initial objections. Not that she normally disagreed with him, but she'd been adamant. She might be marrying a man her father had chosen for her, but it was *her* wedding, after all.

Suddenly Arden became acutely aware of the scent of Christmas wreaths and pinecones and the fragrance of candles in the church that had been decorated for the holiday. Outside, snow lingered on the stained-glass windows before sliding out of sight. She could hear the shuffling feet of the choir as it assembled to help celebrate her wedding.

They were sounds and scents she'd experienced all her life. But she'd never sensed them so acutely before. And never had she felt so intimidated by them.

She heard her parents' voices as they opened the door to join her.

"Well, daughter, you certainly look beautiful today!" Hiram Crandall, resplendent in his ministerial robes, beamed at her as they entered. "Your mother and I are proud of you. And John, too, of course," he added as an afterthought.

"Oh, Hiram, do you remember when I wore that wedding dress the day you and I were married?" Tears of happiness formed in Louise Crandall's eyes as she gingerly embraced her daughter. "Take good care of the dress, honey. I know you'll want your own daughter to wear it someday."

Arden gritted her teeth and tried to smile. The white velvet sheath with its lace inserts was lovely. But it wasn't the dress she would have chosen for herself. The silk taffeta bridal creation with flowing detachable train that she'd originally chosen still hung in the bridal salon.

"Now, Louise. You're being a bit premature, aren't you?" Arden's father chided gently. "Arden has to learn to be a good wife before she can be a good mother."

He turned to Arden and took her hand. "We've come to give you our blessings and our advice, daughter. Cleave to your husband. Trust him to lead you to a full and rewarding life. And don't forget all that your mother and I have taught you."

With these admonitions, he kissed Arden's brow, took his teary wife's arm and turned to leave. "John is waiting to join us at the altar. I shall be back to walk you down the aisle as soon as I've seated your mother." He glanced at his watch. "I expect I'll be ready to perform the ceremony in about ten minutes."

At their exit, Arden felt the door to her freedom close behind them. Her father's words had sounded like a jail sentence instead of a blessing. A benevolent jail, but a jail nevertheless.

She tried to picture married life with John Travers. John was a good man, but he was a younger version of her father: staid and conservative. The knowledge that she was marrying him because her father had urged the marriage on her didn't help settle the queasy feeling deep in her middle. Or the uneasy feeling that she was going from one set of paternal hands to another.

She'd been living at home at her father's request. After all, he'd reminded her, she had to be an example for the other young women in her father's congregation. But she was twenty-two years old and financially independent because of the wise investments she'd made. She had a mind of her own and dreams, as well, although she had too much respect for her father to voice them. Now she was being told to let her future husband think for her and guide her! Knowing John as well as she did, she wasn't sure he was the one to lead her into a full and exciting life.

Just the thought of the predictable, structured future awaiting her under John's guidance was terrifying. Instead, she tried to concentrate on the honeymoon ahead of her: the clear, blue waters of the Gulf of Mexico; the white sandy beaches of Cancún she'd seen in travel brochures. And John Travers as her husband.

That didn't help much, either. As John's wife she would never be allowed to be her own woman.

She shivered.

"My goodness! Your hands are ice-cold! John isn't going to like that one bit." Margo's smile faded as she noted her friend's pale complexion and heard her faint moan.

Arden scarcely listened. She was remembering her father's parting comments.

"Come on, Arden," Margo said as she added a touch of rouge to Arden's cheeks. "John's really a great guy. A bit stuffy, but all he needs is to be shown how to loosen up. I envy you, I really do.''

Arden didn't feel any better after Margo's comments. If anyone could get John to loosen up, it would be someone like Margo, not her.

The organ music coming through the door paused and slowly changed to the wedding march. A discreet knock sounded at the door. Her father!

She froze.

Chapter One

"Attention. Your attention please." Loudspeakers blared over the tumult in the terminal. "All flights in and out of JFK continue to be on hold. The State of New York regrets any inconvenience this delay may have caused."

On hold. Luke McCauley grimaced as he shook off the layer of snow that clung to the shoulders of his heavy woolen overcoat. He followed a group being led by a tour leader carrying a sign that said: Majestic Honeymoon Express. Although the Majestic charter plane was his destination, he wasn't on a honeymoon, thank God. Still, it was a good cover. Alone, he would have stood out like a sore thumb. Ambling along with the honeymooners, he merely felt like a fool, under the shower of rice and confetti being thrown by well-wishers.

The three-day storm that had closed the JFK airport was tapering off, but the ice and snow falling from the terminal overhang was a pretty good indication that planes wouldn't be departing anytime soon. A delay in his departure was the last thing he needed or wanted.

His no-nonsense reputation as a top secret service agent had kept him constantly in demand and on the move. Now that he had resigned to work freelance, he still wasn't free of the scent of danger that followed him.

He'd taken this last job and wanted to get it over as quickly as possible so he could get on with his life. The holster, now empty, that hung from his shoulder had become as much a part of him as his left arm. Security would return his gun to him in Cancún. The license that gave him the right to carry it had been heavily scrutinized. An old story.

Even so, he knew without being told there were watchful eyes on him. Nowadays, men who carried guns were suspect.

"Merry Christmas!" someone shouted, throwing mistletoe in the air.

"You, too," Luke muttered. Though it was tomorrow, Christmas was just another day on the calendar for him. A guy in his line of business didn't have much time for sentiment.

He glanced at the shops gaily decorated for the holiday. "White Christmas" was playing on someone's boom box. It sure was a white Christmas, he thought, remembering the six-foot-deep ice- and snowbank he'd fought his way through to get into the terminal. With luck, this snowstorm would be the last one he would have to experience.

The pressure of a handcuff reminded him of the briefcase chained to his wrist. He'd been roped into delivering it to the owners of the Majestic Hotel in Cancún as soon as possible. An awkward arrangement, it made him feel and look like a criminal. It was the last thing he needed, but maybe it would accomplish the purpose he had in mind.

He'd tried to avoid the antiquated arrangement, arguing that a briefcase chained to his wrist was outdated, outmoded and sure as hell asking for trouble. But the new foreign owners of the hotel had refused to consider electronic mail or wire transfers, firm in their belief that the contents of the briefcase could somehow be stolen or go astray. No amount of pleading had cut it.

In his breast pocket was a round-trip ticket on the honeymoon charter flight of the Majestic-owned airlines. He was the only one who knew he might not be on its return flight.

As he moved through the crowd, he could see that the waiting area was full of additional honeymoon couples headed for the warm sands and turquoise waters of the Mexican Caribbean. As for himself, he figured he'd probably be single for the rest of his life. No woman in her right mind would put up with his spur-of-the-moment schedule. Not that he was interested in settling down, anyway.

The pressure of the handcuff that reminded him of the briefcase's valuable contents was beginning to rile him. For a while now he'd been thinking he was plain nuts for helping other people get rich. Wasn't it long past time for him to think about feathering his own nest?

A lone woman in the group caught his eye. He'd heard all brides were beautiful and looked radiant on their wedding day. The bride that caught his eye, as he made his way through the milling crowd, was beautiful, but definitely not radiant. She looked as dejected and wilted as the bedraggled bouquet of white and red roses she held in one hand. A Majestic Honeymoon Tour bag hung from her wrist. In her other hand, she clutched the handle to her suitcase. The wedding dress he glimpsed under her long black raincoat was wet and muddy. Her white satin shoes looked as though she'd tramped through every puddle in New York City.

On closer scrutiny, her blond hair was damp. Tendrils had curled around a pale, cream-colored complexion. Her expressive blue eyes were clouded as she gazed unhappily around her. She had full, curved lips that begged to be kissed. A pity, he thought fleetingly. Even in her disarray, she looked charming. A tiny flame of desire kindled within him. Foolish, he knew, since it was obvious she'd just been married, and he had something more important on his mind.

But any woman who was as eye-catching as this one surely deserved a better beginning to her wedded life than this.

He paused only momentarily as he strode to the gate to check in for his flight. His first priorities were minding his own business and taking care not to draw attention to himself. Unhappy females were not. Whatever the bride's problems, he figured they were her husband's responsibility, not his.

Except that she looked particularly miserable, and too beautiful to be alone on her wedding day.

His thoughts turned to a more pleasurable subject. His future. This was his chance to get out of the trying and sometimes dark world he moved in. A chance to kick back and indulge in a fantasy or two. To do the things he'd never had the time or money to do—before tonight.

The bride caught up with him at the Majestic Airlines gate. As Luke took his place in the line of impatient travelers, he noticed her wiping away drops that were sliding down her cheeks. Tears at a time like this?

He glanced around the waiting area but didn't see an unattached male anywhere. Idly he wondered if there was more to the bride's problem than he thought. For instance, just where was her groom?

ARDEN CRANDALL SNIFFED as she reached into the pocket of her damp raincoat and extracted a limp tissue. She gazed around the waiting area where newly wedded couples were passing the time cuddling. The enormity of what she'd done finally hit her. She was not only heading into the unknown, she was headed there alone.

She'd expected to feel happy with her decision to start a new life without a husband's guiding hand. To be independent, to make her own decisions and to search for excitement. Especially without a husband whose idea of adventure was a potluck supper.

She'd looked forward to traveling to Mexico. The pictures in magazines and colorful brochures depicting clear water and pristine sands had promised so much. Instead, she was stuck in a cold airport and becoming colder and more miserable by the minute.

The public address system came alive again.

"Attention. Your attention please," the disembodied voice announced. "We regret to inform you that all incoming and outgoing flights continue to be on hold. We will keep you posted for further developments."

Arden groaned. The "storm of the century" that blanketed the entire northeast coast had created an unexpected ending to an escape that had begun with promise. She'd hoped to be in the air winging her way to a new life by now. Every minute she remained in the airport was another opportunity for her fiancé or her father to catch up with her.

She worried her lips and pulled her wet raincoat closer. The velvet wedding dress should have kept her warm, but tonight it wasn't enough. Not that the rest of her clothing in her suitcase could afford her any comfort. The sundresses, skimpy cotton shorts, tops and bikini bathing suits were meant for the warm beaches of Cancún, not the cold departure gates of JFK. She was stuck wearing her wedding dress and a raincoat whose dampness reminded her of how miserable she felt. If there was any warmth in the terminal, she couldn't feel it.

"Attention, everyone. May I have your attention, please. I have the latest departure information for you," the Majestic counter agent announced over the loud speaker. Voices stilled. Arden's heart sank even lower as she listened.

"Sorry, folks," the agent went on. "It looks as if you're not going to be able to go anywhere for a while. I'll let you know when we're cleared for departure, but with the runways covered with snow and ice, I doubt it will be anytime soon.''

"But it's my wedding night!" a dismayed bride cried.

"Don't worry, sweetheart," her husband said soothingly. "We'll spend the night in a local hotel."

"How about putting all of us up in a hotel?" a strident male voice called.

The harried agent shook her head. "According to our latest information, all the hotels in New York City and surrounding areas are full to capacity. As a matter of fact, I hear people are even sleeping in hotel lobbies. I'm afraid you'll have to make yourselves as comfortable as you can right here in the airport."

"How about some pillows and blankets?"

"We'll see what we can do, but no promises," the attendant answered frankly. "None of us anticipated this emergency."

A collective groan arose from her listeners.

"It's a heck of a way to spend Christmas Eve," a disgruntled passenger commented, "and a worse way to spend a wedding night."

Arden glanced at her watch. The six o'clock departure time for Cancún had long since come and gone. Even a hotel lobby would have been welcome. She wrapped her arms around herself trying to keep warm.

Her envious gaze fell on a man across from her. In his heavy coat, woolen scarf and leather gloves, he looked a lot warmer than she was. He was sitting on the floor, leaning against a small overnight bag.

Their eyes met. Arden shivered again when she noticed the faded scar that ran under his lower lip. Shivers that not only came from the cold but from an involuntary awareness of his dark and dangerous male appearance. He looked larger than life and resembled the heroes in the latest action movies: all brawn and ready to use it. The expression in his piercing eyes that matched the color of his sable hair was frankly appraising.

The briefcase that was chained to the man's wrist gave her something to think about. He was a man she instinctively felt would spell trouble—and she wasn't looking for any more trouble than she already had.

He was totally unlike her fiancé and the other men she'd met. She swallowed hard.

Although she managed an impersonal smile in response to the lop-sided one that briefly curved at his lips when their eyes met, she looked away before he could interpret it as an invitation to start a conversation.

To add to her distress, the sound of traditional Christmas carols wafted through the air from a boom box held by one of the passengers. It reminded her it was her first Christmas Eve away from her family.

Throughout the terminal, many of the travelers on their way home for Christmas carried brightly wrapped packages. The airport shops sparkled with colored holiday lights, wreaths, ornaments and holiday greetings. Even the Majestic gate attendants wore Santa Claus hats that jingled every time they moved.

Although snow was piled high on the terminal's skylights, the holiday excitement in the air belied the cold reality of the storm outside the terminal. Even the

air seemed heavy with the fresh scent of Christmas
trees.

She sank deeper into her raincoat, her spirits dropping as fast as the temperature around her.

She was struck with a heavy sense of guilt at leaving her family and her fiancé on a night like tonight.
Not only was it Christmas Eve, she thought wearily,
tonight was to have been her wedding night. Maybe
if she'd been able to see John as a more exciting man
and less of a father figure, he would have been beside
her.

"Attention. Your attention please," a voice commanded over the airport loud speakers. "Due to the
unexpected demand for refreshments and the conces-
sionaire's inability to restock supplies under the present conditions, all food concessions will close in ap-
proximately twenty minutes."

As if on cue, hordes of passengers rushed to the
food concessions. She wasn't in the mood for airport
food, Arden mused wistfully. Not when she remembered the glazed ham and plum pudding her mother
had prepared for her wedding reception. What she did
need was enough hot coffee to see herself through the
night.

All around her, honeymoon couples were taking the
opportunity to cuddle a little closer. The cold, hard
stone bench she'd chosen as a place of refuge was a
constant reminder this was no place to be spending
Christmas Eve by herself, surrounded by people she'd
never seen before. Being frankly studied by the dark
stranger facing her wasn't doing much for her peace
of mind, either.

"Excuse me, but are you alone?"

Arden came to with a start. A young couple had seated themselves beside her. When she got Arden's attention, the woman smiled.

"I'm Judith Smith, and this is my husband, Jeremy. We're on our honeymoon, too," she said with a coy smile at the man seated beside her. "I couldn't help but notice your own husband isn't with you. I thought perhaps he may have stepped away for a moment, so I hesitated to say anything until now."

"I don't have a husband," Arden automatically responded before she realized it wasn't a good idea to tell the truth at a time like this. And especially to strangers. "That is," she amended, "he'll be along soon."

"Dear me," the woman laughed. "I'll bet there's a story behind that one. Don't you think so, Jeremy?" Her husband nodded.

"Not really," Arden replied politely. She wasn't about to share her story with a stranger, no matter how friendly. As far as anyone was concerned, she *was* waiting for her husband to join her.

How could she tell anyone that only a few hours ago she'd been on the verge of marrying the very proper John Travers? A man she'd known for years and the man her minister father had chosen for her? And that the opening strains of the wedding march had sent her rushing from the church?

"But you're still going on a honeymoon?"

"Yes, of course," Arden assured her. "My husband has stepped away for a little while. He'll be back before the plane leaves." Apprehensive at the thought that John might actually show up, she glanced around the waiting area. The last thing she wanted was for him to turn up looking for her.

"Good for you. I'm sure he'll show up soon," Judith Smith soothed. "I certainly wish you both well."

The terminal loudspeaker blared again. "Your attention, your attention, please. All food concessions will be closing in ten minutes."

Arden stirred uneasily. She wanted a cup of hot coffee more than ever, but the prospect of dragging her belongings with her to the food concession area was daunting.

"Something wrong?" Judith Smith inquired.

"I was just wishing I could go and get some hot coffee while I still can. But I don't see how I can manage if I have to take my luggage with me," Arden answered, glancing at her purse, suitcase and flight bag. "I guess I should have checked it through to Cancún, but I was running late. I didn't want to miss the plane."

"Oh, is that all? My husband and I will be happy to watch your things for you."

Arden hesitated only a moment. Surely her luggage would be safe with someone going on the same flight with her.

"Thanks a million," she said, gathering her purse. "I'll be right back. Can I bring you anything?"

"No, thank you. We're doing just fine." Judith Smith winked at her husband. "Aren't we, Jeremy?"

"You bet!" he agreed. "Go on. Judith and I don't mind doing you a favor. Especially on a night like this."

Arden walked down the corridor to join a long line of weary travelers waiting for any food that might still be available. That there was a Good Samaritan to be found on Christmas Eve didn't surprise her. As the daughter of a minister, she'd heard the story often enough. That she should find one amongst strangers in an airport waiting area, willing to guard her luggage, only seemed to make the story more meaningful. If Arden hadn't been so intent on her own thoughts, she might have noticed her Good Samaritan swiftly moving past her line up toward the exit door, carrying her luggage.

A commotion back at the Majestic gate drew her attention. A male voice shouted, "Stop, thief!"

Arden craned to see what was happening. A man came barreling down the hall with a security guard hard on his heels. Strangely enough, it was the mysterious man with whom she'd exchanged impersonal smiles a short time ago.

Another airport security guard materialized behind him in no time. As the three ran toward her, her heart began to beat wildly. Something about the way they were eyeing her told her she was about to be involved in whatever was going on.

"Come with me!" the dark stranger shouted at her. He barely paused before he reached for her arm and tried to pull her along with him. "I'll need you to identify your luggage!"

"*My* luggage?" Bewildered at the commotion, and not all that convinced the man was someone she should follow, Arden clutched her purse and pulled out of his grasp. She had no idea who he was—maybe he was a thief himself. After all, he had that briefcase chained to his wrist. *Someone* didn't think he was all that trustworthy.

She dug in her heels. "I'm not going anywhere with you! Officer," she called over her shoulder with as much dignity as she could muster with him tugging at her arm and his briefcase banging against her hip. "This man is annoying me with a story about my luggage being stolen. I don't believe him! I'd appreciate your coming back with me to where I left it."

"You left your luggage unattended?" her would-be rescuer muttered, his expression incredulous. "No wonder someone grabbed a chance to take it."

"Not at all," Arden answered with a dark look. "I left it back at the Majestic gate with a very nice couple on the same tour as I am. I'm sure we'll find them and my luggage just where I left it."

Luke groaned as he searched the crowded terminal. The couple escaping with her luggage was out of sight. Considering the thousands of people holed up in JFK for the last three days, his chances of finding them were slim to none. Or, as his grandfather would say, his chances were "about as great as a snowball in hell."

"Have it your way," he said, giving up the argument. He let go of her arm and stood back. He was resigned to the loss of the luggage. After all, it wasn't his, and he'd tried to do the right thing. If anyone had a problem, it was her. How would the lonesome bride feel when she found out her luggage was actually gone?

He followed the bride and the two security guards

back to the Majestic departure area. A trail of curiosity seekers followed him. In a short time, to his disgust, it began to look like a parade.

Sure enough, the bench where he'd last seen the solitary bride and her luggage was empty. That didn't come as a big surprise. Not to him; not when he'd already caught a glimpse of the "honeymoon couple" disappearing into the crowded terminal with the bride's luggage. If she'd only cooperated instead of dragging her heels, the outcome might have been different.

"They're gone!" Arden cried. "And they've taken my luggage with them!"

"Who's they?" the security guard inquired. "Someone you know?"

"Yes. That is, no," she answered as she searched the curious onlookers for a familiar face. Her heart sank when she realized she'd been taken by thieves. "But they seemed so friendly. They even gave me their names!"

"Yeah?" the officer said as he took out a small notebook and a pencil and prepared to take notes. "Who did they say they were?"

"Judith and Jeremy Smith."

Luke groaned. "Smith," he echoed, shaking his head. Even a rank amateur could have sensed it wasn't the couple's real name. "Where in heaven's name did you come from not to have realized those were phony names? Another planet?"

"No," Arden replied, beginning to get angry at his tone. "But as long as you're asking, where I *do* come from, nothing like this would have happened."

But the man was right. Thinking back over the night's events, Arden wasn't so sure she'd acted intelligently. Especially by trusting in strangers. What she didn't need was someone rubbing it in; she felt bad enough already. Things were going from bad to worse, sure, but there wasn't any use crying over them now.

"Then you should have done yourself a favor and stayed there," he said, pragmatically. "This is the big city. The Smiths and people like them are just lying in wait for someone like you. Especially on a night like this."

"I'm afraid the guy's right," the security guard interjected. "If you had any valuables in your suitcase and want to file a report, follow me. I'll see what I can do. But personally, I think you can kiss your luggage goodbye."

"I didn't have anything really valuable in there, just some trousseau things. Just warm-weather clothing," Arden said with a sigh. "But I would like to file a report. I'd hate to let them get away without putting the theft and their descriptions on record." She nodded coolly to the dark stranger, who continued to assess her steadily. She didn't need a crystal ball to know he considered her naive. And from the look on his face, maybe even stupid.

"How about you, sir?" the security officer continued, with a sharp glance at Luke. "Care to come along as a witness to the crime?"

Luke thought rapidly. If he'd wanted to keep a low profile, this wasn't the way to do it. One question would only lead to another. Especially with the officer eyeing the chain dangling from his wrist.

"No, thanks," Luke said hastily. "I'll be around. You can call on me if you catch up with the thieves and want me to identify them."

"Got a reason for that handcuff?" the officer asked casually as he put the notebook back in his breast pocket.

"Yeah," Luke answered shortly. "I'm a courier."

"You don't say," the officer answered sharply, glancing at the slight bulge over Luke's left breast. "Got a license to carry that?"

"It's an empty holster. I checked the gun," Luke said wearily. He was used to the question-and-answer routine, but he liked it less and less as time went on.

"Mind if I take a look?"

"Not at all." Luke unbuttoned his overcoat long enough for the guard to check the empty holster.

"So, you're making a delivery?" the uniformed man said, motioning his head for Luke to button up.

"Yeah. If the airport runways ever thaw out."

"Well, good luck," the officer said as he turned to leave. "You're going to need it. But be careful, there are a lot of shady characters around the airport tonight."

"So I've heard," Luke replied, mindful that the man's look included him. "And I think I just met a couple of them a few minutes ago."

ARDEN WAS THE FOCUS of attention for a few minutes, until the novelty of the situation wore off and the honeymooners went back to finding their own ways to keep warm. Envious in spite of herself, and colder than ever, she soon found herself with only her wounded ego to keep her warm. Tears of frustration began to gather at the back of her eyes.

"Here," a voice said. "Maybe this will help." A tanned hand offered her a cup of black coffee. She glanced up into the dark eyes of its donor.

It was the mystery man.

She took the drink only because she was cold, she told herself. The coffee, his enigmatic expression and assessing eyes warmed her middle. Her pulse stepped up its beat. Never had her erstwhile fiancé affected her this way.

She stole a glance at the handcuff on his wrist. How did she know he hadn't been an accomplice of the Smiths? Maybe he'd tried to create a diversion so they could get away? After all, no one else but him had noticed the theft in progress. And he *had* given up the chase much too easily when the security officers caught up with him.

"Thank you," she said, wiping away a tear that hung at the corner of her eye.

"Here," he said as he offered her a clean handkerchief. "No use crying. Not now."

"Thank you, but I never cry," she replied, taking the handkerchief and putting it to work.

"Really? You could have fooled me. Most women would have been crying their eyes out by now. At a time like this, I'd feel pretty miserable myself if the theft had happened to me."

"Maybe you're just lucky," she replied as she settled back on the stone bench.

"Not so lucky," he answered ruefully. "After all, I'm stuck here in an airport terminal on Christmas Eve with nowhere to go, just like everyone else."

Arden had to agree. Christmas Eve was for families, for going to church and exchanging gifts. Despite the decorations and the Christmas carols on the boom box, tonight wasn't the holiday she loved. For better or worse, if she hadn't panicked at the sound of the wedding march, she could have at least been sharing tonight's experience with her new husband.

Except the picture of the husband that formed in her mind wasn't that of John. It was of the dark man in front of her!

She held the hot cup the stranger gave her in two hands to keep warm. The pungent odor of the freshly brewed coffee and its warmth reminded her she at least owed him common courtesy for the coffee, if nothing else. She ventured a smile.

"I have to believe the Smiths were right about one thing," he went on. "Your being here alone and in a wedding dress must have quite a story behind it."

"You listened to our conversation?" Arden sputtered. Her gratitude abruptly vanished. "Why didn't you say something to warn me when you had the chance?"

"You were all getting along so famously, I figured you must know them. It wasn't until you disappeared that I realized the guy had his hand on your luggage and she was holding your flight bag. By the time I got to my feet they were on their way."

"Well," Arden said glancing philosophically at her purse, "at least I have my traveler's checks. Not that

I relish the prospect of having to wear my wedding dress and raincoat all night. But I guess clothes can be replaced when I get to Cancún.''

She looked away, pretending he wasn't there. Luke wasn't fooled. She might act cool, but she was as much interested in him as he was with her. Under his amused gaze, a blush appeared on her face. He was sure of it when a dimple danced across her cheek.

''Why don't you come over here and sit down beside me until your husband arrives,'' he offered, taken by an impulse. ''That is, *if* you have a husband.'' He pointedly glanced at her ringless left hand.

''I do,'' she answered, hiding her hand in the folds of her raincoat. ''He's out looking for the taxicab we arrived in. I inadvertently left our travel documents in there.''

''We can keep each other warm until he comes back,'' he offered. Luke would have bet a hundred she was on the honeymoon tour alone. He dropped to the small place he'd staked out against the wall and made room beside him.

''I promise not to take advantage of the situation,'' he said solemnly when she hesitated. He loosened his woolen scarf and threw open his heavy overcoat. Underneath, he was dressed in a conservative brown business suit, white shirt, a vest and a paisley tie. He tucked the briefcase behind him and pulled the sleeve of his overcoat over his left wrist. That ought to reassure her, he thought as he watched changing expressions run across her face. They went from ''no'' to ''maybe.'' ''Come on,'' he coaxed, ''I'm willing to share. And I don't bite.''

Arden was tempted. The man appeared to be everything she'd dreamed about when she'd become old enough to dream: ruggedly handsome, confident and with an air of mystery about him; the exact opposite of everything she'd been taught to want by her father. In her present mood that was enough to cause her to consider going into his arms.

"How come you're dressed for the storm?" she asked as she fought temptation. "Most everyone else is wearing wedding attire or resort things under their raincoats."

"Simple," he answered blandly. "I don't plan on remaining in Cancún. I intend to take the next flight back to New York."

Arden glanced at the honeymoon couple seated alongside him. The bride was fast asleep in her husband's arms and looked a lot warmer than Arden did.

She still hesitated. Her circumspect upbringing and her job as a church secretary seemed light-years away from the position she found herself in now. Cuddling with a strange man wasn't something she'd ever considered. Until now.

She hadn't been raised as a minister's daughter for nothing, Arden reflected as she considered his offer. She might be a late-blooming rebel, but her strict upbringing had left its mark.

Who was this man? What was he up to? And what guarantee did she have that he'd keep his promise not to try to take advantage of the situation?

Arden could still hear her minister father's voice thundering in her ears as she fled the church, warning her of dire consequences for her behavior. For a fleeting moment she wondered what he would say if he knew what she was contemplating doing now.

After a moment of shivering reflection, Arden decided that since her father wasn't here to pass judgment on her decision, she'd take this man up on his offer. She might feel guilty over the mess she'd made of her wedding day, but not enough to punish herself by sitting on a cold, hard, stone bench all night. Besides, what her father didn't know couldn't bother him.

She wondered what it would be like to spend a few hours in this man's arms. The dangerous edge to him she sensed when she'd first gazed at him continued to attract her in a way John's appearance had never done.

Maybe it had been her fault. Margo had kept telling her to loosen up and smell the roses, but she'd been conditioned too well by her Victorian father. Poor John. Maybe she hadn't given him any encouragement to be anything other than a proper suitor.

It looked as if things were going to change.

This afternoon she'd run for her life from her own wedding. Now she was contemplating doing something completely out of character.

Was this man part of the independence, the adventure, the excitement she'd set her heart on finding? Was it wise, or even safe, to accept his invitation? His sure, steady gaze seemed to dare her to take a chance.

It was that dare that made her consider his offer.

She tried to resist temptation and failed miserably. With a mental admonition to be on her guard, she decided to take him up on his offer.

She resolutely tossed what was left of her bridal

bouquet into the trash container beside her. And with it she threw away the last reminder of her guilt. After twenty-two years of listening to her father's advice, it was time to think for herself.

If she was on the road to hell, as her father had predicted, she intended to enjoy the ride.

Chapter Two

"I'd like to know your name."

"McCauley," he answered, after a moment of hesitation.

"That's all?" At least she should know the first name of the man whose arms would be around her, Arden thought.

"Luke," he added reluctantly, "and that's all you need to know about me right now," he answered. "By the way, what's yours?"

"Arden Crandall," she answered.

"Miss?"

"Of course not!" she replied. She shot him a defiant look that defied him to doubt her. He smiled a wicked smile that sent another unexpected shiver through her. But she knew she was going to take him up on his offer. There *was* that glint in his challenging eyes that drew her.

A dare was a dare.

"Thank you, I will take you up on your offer," Arden answered. She glanced around to see if anyone was paying attention to them or looked as if they cared. Thankfully, the unaccustomed accommodations had taken its toll. She was surrounded by couples settling down to make the best of a bad situation. A few die-hards were still awake and exchanging hugs and kisses. She hurriedly closed the distance between herself and her rescuer. Once beside him, she nestled into his warmth.

The coat he pulled over her smelled of rain and fresh snow. The tanned cheek resting against her hair smelled faintly of seductive shaving lotion. The arms that held her were strong and sure. And, to her secret satisfaction, that air of danger that fascinated her still clung to him.

This man was nothing like her fiancé. John, who at thirty-eight was sixteen years older than she, had kissed her as if he were afraid she would break. She'd felt a vague dissatisfaction with his embraces, but hadn't known why. Until now.

She tried to relax. In this man's arms, her thoughts turned to Cancún, to the Majestic Resort at the tip of the Yucatan Peninsula of Mexico where she was headed. She pictured bronze, muscular Indian males and exotic maidens with flowing, black tresses. Of warm, tropical breezes and sandy beaches. The mental images made her feel strangely happy and contented.

Come to think of it, she thought with a smile, the man who held her in his strong arms made her feel pretty good, too.

In a wild burst of imagination, she pictured him beside her on a chalk white beach wearing a brief bikini. The sun would shoot glints of gold into his sable hair. His dark eyes would be warm and soft as he turned his inviting gaze on her and opened his arms.

She envisioned herself going eagerly into his embrace, her flesh burning under his hands.

Arden stifled a giggle. She had to stop this before her imagination carried her into dangerous waters. She didn't know anything about the man who held her, and yet she was picturing honeymooning with him. She sighed wistfully as she snuggled closer to his muscular chest. Dreams were okay when there was nothing else to look forward to, but the real thing felt definitely better.

"Here, why don't you take off your wet raincoat and try to relax?" Luke asked, as he became aware of the cold sweeping through him.

She shook her head.

"Why not? I would think you'd be a lot more comfortable without it."

"I'm afraid it might turn up missing," she explained. "It's the only thing I have left besides this dress."

"Is that the only reason? Or don't you want me to see what the rest of you looks like?" he teased. He figured he might as well make a joke of it. It was obviously going to be the only way a skittish Arden Crandall was going to remain within a foot of him without that damn raincoat that was sending chills through him. And even that distance might be too far away, now that he was surprised to discover how much he enjoyed having her in his arms.

The awareness of how much he actually enjoyed having her beside him began to trouble him, but not enough to call her off. There was time enough for that later.

"Not at all," she replied. "I'm just an ordinary woman. I'm certain you've seen a woman in a bridal outfit before."

"True," he answered. But she wasn't an ordinary bride, not without a bridegroom. "But from what I can tell, your raincoat isn't doing you any good and it's making *me* cold."

"Oh. I'm sorry. I guess I wasn't thinking." She reached for her belt buckle, then hesitated. The searching look she was giving him was enough to make a hardened criminal confess to crimes he hadn't even gotten around to yet. What did she think he was going to do? Ravish her?

"What's the matter now?"

"Like I said, I'd hate to lose the raincoat."

"If you're that afraid, why don't you turn it inside out and sit on it?"

"Good idea," she answered. Her eyes lit up. "Let me go for a minute, and I'll take care of it."

"Sure," Luke answered. He threw open his woolen overcoat with his free right hand, taking care to keep his handcuffed left wrist hidden in its folds. The last thing he wanted was for that fool handcuff on his wrist to spook her.

He hated to let her go, even for a few minutes. He didn't really understand why, he reflected, as he watched her struggle with her damp raincoat. He'd only laid eyes on her a few hours ago.

His half-formulated plans were still unsettled. A couple of disgruntled individuals were on the loose, eager to get even with him. Under the circumstances, a romantic entanglement at Cancún was the last thing he needed or wanted. But there was something about her that made him want to hold her a little tighter, a little longer.

Maybe because tonight was Christmas Eve he'd had an attack of nostalgia, and she represented a human awareness or a warmth he'd missed out on until now—things he hadn't gotten around to wanting because of the life he'd led. But when he was with Arden, her touch was something he suddenly seemed to need.

He stirred uneasily. No way was he going to let his thoughts drift in that direction. He had more important things to think about.

His life had become pretty tiresome. Not that anyone besides himself thought so. Everyone who knew him thought his work was mysterious and fascinating. Some even envied him. If they only knew. He'd been shot at, mugged, arrested, fingerprinted, jailed and released more times than he cared to count.

At thirty-two, he'd had enough. Living on the edge had become wearing. And not very lucrative financially, everything considered. He'd helped a lot of people to get their just deserts, and some even became rich in spite of it. Maybe now was the time to think of feathering his own nest with the means he had in his grasp.

He thought of being in some faraway place he could call his own. Of waking up in the same bed for days at a time. Of not having to look over his shoulder. And never having to take another job like this one for the rest of his life.

When Arden had made herself comfortable, nestling herself back into his side, his thoughts turned back to

her. The white velvet wedding dress clung to her figure in a way that made him envy her absent husband—
if she had one.

Marriage might be okay for her, but not for him.
Especially now that he was on the verge of making a
decision he couldn't ask a woman to share.

He waited patiently until she made herself comfortable, then he pulled his heavy woolen overcoat over
them.

"Better?" he asked. He was rewarded by a contented murmur. The pressure of her slender form
against his engendered a protective feeling that surprised him. And even scared him, now that he had a
chance to think of it. He hoped he wasn't creating any
complications for himself.

"So," he continued, loath to be left alone with his
thoughts. "What are you doing here?"

"You already know that," she answered with a
yawn. "I'm on my honeymoon."

Luke had already decided Arden might not have
told the Smiths the real story, or he wouldn't have
invited her to share his warmth. He'd come to the
conclusion she was on the Majestic Honeymoon Tour
dressed as a bride for a publicity stunt or maybe for a
magazine shoot. Now that she'd actually reiterated her
story about being on a honeymoon, his good humor
plummeted like an express elevator. Considering how
he'd been taken by her, it was just as well she was
definitely off-limits. He looked cautiously around him.

"So, where's this groom of yours?"

He gently shifted her weight from his shoulder. If
an irate groom or someone with a grudge did show up

and decide to take a shot at him, he didn't stand a prayer of defending himself. Not with her plastered to his chest and in the line of fire. He damned himself for not thinking of the possibility before this.

"He's not back yet." She sniffed into his chest and wiped the tip of her nose with her fist. "I think I'm catching a cold." Unable to reach the handkerchief she'd returned to him, he handed her the corner of his scarf.

"How about running that by me one more time? Back from where?"

"He's out trying to find the taxicab we came in," she answered. "I inadvertently left our travel documents in there."

"What do you think his chances are of finding the right cab on a night like this?" he asked, swallowing his laughter.

Arden shrugged. She wasn't about to tell him that the last time she saw John he was standing at the church altar waiting for her to come down the aisle. Better to let him think John would eventually show up.

"You're sure you want to stick to that story?" he asked.

Arden nodded. He probably thought she was out of her mind, she thought as she burrowed closer to his warmth. After what she'd put herself through the past few hours and the unknown that loomed ahead of her, she was beginning to think so, too.

"Of course," Luke assured her, "strange things happen all the time. Some more strange than others.

But in my experience, I've found there's usually a story behind them.''

She listened to his reassuring, steady heartbeat, fighting off the temptation to tell him her story. There *was* that mysterious take-charge aura surrounding him that gave her confidence, made her feel he'd be willing to understand if she were to tell him.... But she couldn't.

Arden pretended not to hear. She was going to play dumb. Her reasons for leaving her groom at the altar would probably sound ridiculous to anyone who didn't know John.

She glanced around at her fellow passengers. Wedding bouquets, trailing ribbons and boutonnieres spoke of happy weddings. Bottles of champagne, rice and confetti clinging to hair and clothing spoke of honeymoons and happy endings. She felt a faint pang of regret. Today could have been her own wedding day.

Maybe she'd run because her father had made marriage sound more like a sentence than the start of a new and happy life. When the vestry doors had closed behind him, she'd heard the doors to a more exciting life start to close. It hadn't taken more than the sounds of the wedding march to set her off and running. It was either cut and run or settle for being Mrs. John Travers.

Maybe it *had* been prewedding jitters or stage fright, just as Margo had predicted, but she'd taken one long look through the open vestry door at the altar and hadn't stayed long enough to find out.

There hadn't been anything *really* wrong with John. It was just that she'd realized he had no imagination, no thirst for adventure and that he wouldn't have understood her if she'd tried to explain it to him. He would have been perfectly happy with his nine-to-five job and coming home to his family and television every night.

As for her, she'd been too settled already. It was a joke among her friends that when children from a very strict family broke loose, they broke loose in a big way. She was no exception. She wanted to be independent, live a life of her own and even have an adventure or two rather than watch it on the big screen.

"So what made you and your husband choose Cancún for a honeymoon?"

"It sounded like an adventurous place," she answered, her thoughts still lingering on the scene back at the church.

"What kind of adventures did you have in mind?" Luke inquired politely. Personally, he thought a honeymoon would have been adventure enough for him. Especially with a bride as intriguing as the one he held in his arms.

"I'm not certain, exactly," she answered. "But Cancún seemed to be a good place to start. I'd like to explore the Mayan ruins and spend some time on the other side of the peninsula. I'm sure I could think of something exciting to do after that."

"I?" Luke swallowed a groan. It was obvious she was alone and, perish the thought, he might be stuck with her longer than he'd thought. He'd invited this woman into his arms when his common sense and his need for secrecy should have stopped him. Maybe he shouldn't have been so impulsive.

As for Arden Crandall, did she realize what she was letting herself in for? Did she think there were adventures waiting for her on every corner? If so, she was headed for disappointment. Besides, she might not like the adventures she found—or the ones that found her.

"I hate to ask, since it's none of my business," he said after a slight hesitation. He had to figure out a way to offer her some well-intentioned advice without giving away he knew she was alone.

"I hope you have an income to finance these adventures of yours. They don't come cheap."

"I've been our church secretary for years," she answered confidently. "I've lived at home, saved most of my salary and invested in small companies that have done quite well. I'm going to sell some stock and use the money."

A church secretary? How wealthy or experienced could she be? In his opinion, she was a naive young woman who'd broken loose to become another misguided adventure seeker. Poor soul, Luke decided as he looked down on Arden's glistening curls. Why did everyone else's grass look greener? His was fast becoming nothing more than dirt and dry weeds. The woman in his arms was looking for adventure, just as he'd decided he'd had enough to last him for the rest of his life.

"Is that what you intend to do? Search for a more adventurous life?"

She nodded. "I guess that's part of it."

"And the other part?"

She was too embarrassed to tell him she'd had

enough of being her father's little girl. And that she hadn't wanted to be John's, either.

"I'm not really sure," she answered with a shiver. But she *was* sure.

She'd been afraid of losing her own identity and becoming Mrs. John Travers. And that's why she'd taken off on her own.

She remembered the way her poor mother had cried and how her father had tried to dissuade her when she'd told them she was leaving. She'd already made up her mind. When she grabbed her suitcase and ran out of the vestry, her father was shouting she was on the road to hell. The last she remembered, her mother was sobbing and Margo was jumping up and down, egging her on. And heaven only knew what John was doing back in the church.

She shivered again.

"And this honeymoon you're taking?" he asked, drawing her closer. He told himself he was merely trying to keep her warm, but he had a sinking feeling it was becoming more than that.

In spite of his good intentions to leave well enough alone, her sweet scent filled his senses. Suddenly he wanted to taste her lips, the skin on her soft, velvety neck. The poor groom would never know what he'd missed. "Not many women would have what it takes to see a honeymoon through alone, or to cut all her ties the way you've done."

"I'm not alone!" Arden insisted. "John will be here eventually."

"Yeah, sure," he answered, shifting to a more comfortable position. Thank goodness he knew who he was and where he was headed.

Arden heard the doubt in his voice. But she'd got in so deep, she was beyond caring. She *was* going on a honeymoon, no matter what anyone thought. It was paid for, after all. She had the tour documents in her purse to prove it.

"Actually, I never dreamed I'd end up like this," she murmured, more to herself than him.

"If it's any comfort to you, neither did I," Luke replied as her presence against his chest made itself felt. "Nor," he said glancing over at the sleeping couple beside them, "did anyone else around here."

"I can hardly believe I'm doing this when I don't know you," she confessed wearily, glancing up at Luke. "You may not believe me, but before today, I never would have dreamed of doing anything like this."

"The reason for that's easy," Luke replied with a light laugh. "It hasn't been a normal day for any of us. And as for winding up in my arms, it's because you know you'll never see me again after tonight."

The thought of never seeing Arden Crandall after tonight bothered Luke more than he was willing to admit, even to himself. He was attracted by her gutsy determination to see herself through this so-called adventure of hers. But he had a feeling it was more than that; maybe it was her declaration of independence. Even so, her vulnerability was showing whether or not she realized it. Unless he missed his guess, nothing in her lifestyle had prepared her for the future she envi-

sioned for herself. Not even with money, and especially in a foreign country. What would she do if she
came face-to-face with a real adventure not to her lik-
ing? Who would she turn to if she got in trouble?

His sympathy stirred before he brushed it away.
He'd been trained not to be sympathetic. Still, if ever
a woman needed a helping hand, she did.

He didn't intend to be that helping hand for long.
The most he was prepared to do was keep an eye on
her until they got safely to their destination. He had
his own plans to consider. The last thing he needed
was to be responsible for someone else, now that he
was thinking about changing the direction of his own
future.

She represented an unwelcome tie to his present
identity. An identity he planned to forget after tomorrow.

His thoughts turned to the briefcase. Was his future
already handcuffed to his wrist?

He inhaled Arden's bridal fragrance, the clean smell
of her damp hair where a raindrop or two had found
refuge. Her velvet wedding dress was soft and warm.
She fit into the crook of his arm as naturally as if she
was a part of him. And so was her silken flesh as she
rested her forehead against the side of his neck under
his chin. She was as lovely and refreshing as a spring
flower and different from most of the women he'd
known.

He was actually prepared to enjoy the hours in her
company before they went their separate ways. He'd
never remained in one place long enough to connect
with anyone he was willing to spend the rest of his

life with, this one included. If he carried out his half-formed plans, he'd be home free without anyone to cramp his style.

He shrugged his shoulders and settled back against the wall to wait until the runways were cleared.

Arden shifted uncomfortably as something hard made its presence known against her cheek. Not to mention the something that kept bumping her in the ribs. "For Pete's sake, what *is* that?"

"What is what?" Luke straightened abruptly and looked around him. He relaxed when nothing more than sleeping honeymoon couples caught his eye. From the alarm in her voice, he'd figured maybe her fiancé had actually shown up.

"Whatever it is you have under your left arm," Arden answered. She sat back and stared at him suspiciously. "It feels like a rock!"

"Oh, that," he answered casually as his racing heart slowed down to its normal beat. "That's my holster."

"As in gun?"

"To be truthful with you, yes."

"Loaded?" Arden asked apprehensively.

"I could hardly be carrying a gun in an airport, now could I? Besides, what would be the point of carrying a gun if it weren't loaded?" Luke asked. How naive could a woman get?

She did a double take, until she evidently decided he was joking.

"Did you ever shoot anyone?"

"Only when they deserved it," he answered shortly. He'd had enough of her probing into his private life.

He eyed her in a way calculated to shut her up. It didn't.

She moved another inch away from him and studied him thoughtfully.

"Who *are* you, anyway?" she finally asked. Her eyes widened, her breath caught in her throat, as she must have realized she was a little late in asking.

"No one you need to know," he answered. "Why don't you just relax and forget it's there?"

"I can't. Especially with that briefcase banging into my...and that holster feeling like a rock against my cheek!"

He was more sorry than ever that he'd invited her to share his overcoat. Damn, she was like a puppy worrying a bone.

"Look, think of me as a harmless courier. Nothing more than that."

"Does that account for the briefcase you're carrying?"

"Yep." He was becoming more annoyed by the moment. Not necessarily only at Arden. But at the numskulls at Majestic who should have realized he was bound to attract unwanted attention. It was, after all, a time when computers could accomplish most of what he'd been hired to do. And with a lot less cost and embarrassment to him.

After he'd realized the contents of the suitcase might be the opportunity he'd been waiting for, he couldn't have said no. In hindsight, maybe he should have turned down this particular job and waited for another opportunity. And this time he would ignore anyone who triggered his curiosity.

"What's the matter, don't your employers trust you?" Arden asked, gesturing to the handcuff and chain with distaste.

"Sure they do," he said wearily, shifting his aching back, "or they wouldn't have hired me to deliver it. It's the other guys they don't trust."

"So what's in the briefcase?" she inquired as she rubbed her right side.

"It's not important," Luke answered. Of course he knew, but he wasn't about to tell her.

"Why don't you just unlock the handcuff and put it and the briefcase aside until we leave?" she asked. "It would be a lot more comfortable for you, and for me, too."

"Can't," he replied cryptically.

"Can't or won't?"

"I don't have the key," he answered. "With that said, can we just drop the subject for now?"

She was still eyeing that damn handcuff.

"Come on back here," he said gruffly. He opened his arms.

"Not until I know what's in the briefcase," she announced. "I wouldn't want to get involved in something shady."

Luke bit back the desire to swear.

"Let's just say it's a jackpot and that I can't let it out of my sight," he said impatiently. Much more of this and he'd forget his burst of generosity and send her back to her cold stone bench. For sure, he told himself, it was the last time he intended to get involved in someone else's business.

"It looks uncomfortable. I'll bet it feels uncomfortable, too," she added sourly.

"I intend to get rid of it soon," he said for the last time. "So tell me, are you coming back or not?"

"I suppose so, but I'd appreciate if you'd put that briefcase somewhere where I won't bump into it. The way I feel, I'm going to be black-and-blue by morning."

"Just try not to move and you should be fine," Luke reassured her as he stuffed the briefcase back under his thigh. "It's just a question of mind over matter." He glanced down at Arden as she tried to make herself comfortable. Too bad he couldn't take his own advice. Not only was his mind refusing to function as directed, his physical matter was on full alert.

"Comfortable?" he asked. Arden's curls brushed across his chin as she nodded. He stifled a groan as her perfumed scent wafted past his nose.

Moments after she came back into his arms, he began to regret inviting her. Her enticing scent and her warm breath brushing against his Adam's apple were getting to him. The pressure of her thigh against his sent his more sensitive body parts on fire. He sensed trouble ahead.

As soon as she realized how his body was instinctively reacting to hers, she was bound to figure he was breaking his promise.

Chapter Three

When Luke eased away from her, Arden intuitively sensed something was wrong. She glanced up at his face, where the early signs of a shadow were beginning to show. A frown crinkled his forehead, his lips tightened.

Whatever was bothering him, she hoped it hadn't been something she'd said or done.

"Luke? Is something wrong?" She moved closer, in time to hear a soft sound that sounded like a curse.

She pushed the annoying briefcase away from her hip and reviewed their last verbal exchange.

She'd questioned his identity.

Demanded to know the contents of the briefcase.

Asked if he'd ever killed anyone.

As good as suggested he might be a disreputable character, or worse.

No wonder he didn't want to have anything more to do with her.

But since she had already spent an hour or two in his arms, he should have known she hadn't meant to deliberately hurt or insult him.

Before tonight she'd never known a man like him

whose mere appearance was enough to promise excitement. Naturally, she'd been a little anxious, but her anxiety hadn't changed the way she continued to feel drawn to the mysterious aura that surrounded him.

Without his overcoat covering her, she missed his warmth. And, in a way that might be sinful but was pleasurable all the same, she missed the pressure of his body against hers. He might be all the sins she'd been warned against rolled into one man, but for the first time in her life she didn't care.

If this was the road to hell, so far she was enjoying every mile.

Another glance at Luke showed his dark eyelashes resting on bronze skin. His measured breathing told her he'd fallen asleep. Perhaps she was mistaken about his reasons for moving away and the frustration she'd seen reflected on his face. Maybe he'd been dreaming. And maybe her imagination was working overtime.

She missed being enveloped by his firm arm, missed the male scent that clung to him and the sound of his measured breath against her hair. She moved closer. When her thigh touched his, Luke moved away again, dragging the briefcase with him. She eyed it with distaste, but nestled close.

With a soft groan and a sigh, Luke finally lay still, his head turned away from her.

She could have sworn he shrugged.

Arden waited for him to say something in that full, low voice of his. Instead, his chest rose and fell as if he'd fallen deeper into sleep.

Lucky man, she thought reflectively. There was no

chance she would fall asleep tonight. And not only because of the hard concrete floor under her raincoat.

Luke McCauley's dark masculine presence drew her thoughts down paths she'd been tempted to explore but hadn't until now. And, she thought with a dawning awareness of the growing attraction between them, he was the kind of man she would like to have with her on those paths.

Her eyes burned. As tired as she was, she couldn't sleep. Every time her eyes began to close, she was standing in the vestibule of the church, lifting her skirt with one hand, ready to take the first step down the aisle, and listening to her heart speak the truth.

She gazed at the honeymoon couple asleep next to her. The bridal nosegay had fallen from the bride's hands and was lying on the cold floor between them. A bottle of champagne lay alongside the flowers. Two plastic champagne glasses and a spray of live lilies of the valley were tied to the bottle with festive white ribbons. A small white plastic foam carton had fallen from the bride's lap. Wedding cake, Arden wondered hungrily as she glanced at the carton. Wedding cake to share for good luck on the couple's wedding night?

Awash in nostalgia, she inched her arm from beneath the overcoat and cautiously picked up the bridal bouquet. With a glance at the bride who appeared to be asleep, she buried herself in its fragrance.

The small nosegay was an exquisite study of baby pink and white roses surrounded by delicate maidenhair fern and nestled in a cocoon of a white lace doily. In the center there was a single sweet-smelling gardenia.

Arden sighed into the flower and, for the first time, felt a pang of regret over the day's events. She fingered the open spaces in the white lace doily that framed the tiny roses. Saying the words softly, she recited, "I did the right thing by running away.... Maybe I shouldn't have run away," over and over again. Just as she had chanted as a young girl when she'd played "he loves me, he loves me not" with the petals of daisies.

Luke's voice broke into her litany. "Sorry you walked out on what's-his-name?"

She felt herself blush. He hadn't been asleep, after all. She'd given herself away by her childish game.

"No, not really," she answered truthfully.

They exchanged glances. His steady gaze prompted her to tell him the whole truth. The truth he probably had guessed by now.

"Now that I've given myself away, you might as well know the whole story," she said. "I left because it wouldn't have been fair to go through with the wedding the way I felt about my fiancé."

"Why don't you look at it this way." Luke sighed and straightened up. "Maybe you weren't really in love with the guy."

"You're right. I know that now," Arden replied.

"So how come you were ready to marry him?"

"Actually, I've known John most of my life, and although he's older than I am, we were good friends. My Dad was all for the marriage, and I guess I was trying to please him. It seemed as though it was time for me to get married."

"Time to get married?" Luke shuddered. Marriage

wasn't in the cards for him, nor a long-term relationship, either. Not that he hadn't enjoyed one or two along the way. But if there were a timetable for getting married, he was long overdue. And what's more, he intended to keep it that way.

He stole another glance at Arden, the bridal bouquet in her hands and the bottle of champagne on the floor beside her. There were rose petals in her hair, their faint scent lending her an air of romantic innocence. All things that added up to double trouble. For sure, he was going to have to get out of harm's way pretty soon.

Women today had many choices, he knew, including staying home and raising a family. Just as her fiancé had evidently wanted her to do. His own sister had chosen home, hearth and family and appeared to be very happy. But from what Arden had told him, she hadn't been raised to have many of those other choices. She was no different than he'd been twelve years ago when he'd recognized the smothering existence he was headed for.

Visions of himself as a third generation pharmacist in a small town had been too much for him. He'd opted for a more exciting life, had plunged headlong into danger and been there ever since. But hopefully most of it was behind him. He'd had enough. If only the other players in the games felt the same way.

The question facing Arden, whether she'd stopped to think of it or not, was what was she going to do with the rest of her life after she'd had her own taste of adventure?

Before he had a chance to ask, his attention was diverted.

A jovial voice jolted Luke out of his reverie. "Arden Crandall! What a coincidence to find you here! We thought surely you would be well on your honeymoon by now!"

Arden came to with a start. Dazed, she straightened and looked up at the tall, spare woman with inquisitive eyes who stood there looking down at her. "Aunt Jane?"

"Of course, darling. And here's your Uncle Arthur. Say hello, Arthur!"

Arden drew a ragged breath. All her life she'd been staid and conventional. Out of respect for her parents, she'd kept her dreams to herself. Now, the first time she'd flaunted convention, she'd been caught!

Without waiting for her husband to speak up or for Arden to reply, Jane bubbled on. "I'm sorry we couldn't make it to the wedding ceremony, but the weather held us up. Besides, there were no taxis available and the commuter trains are only running intermittently. So we decided to wait here at the airport until we could take a plane to Florida. We'd planned on going there, anyway. I hear it's nice and warm down there at this time of the year. Well, what's a Christmas without snow? I've tried calling your home for the past few hours, but the line has been busy..."

The speaker's voice trailed off as she finally noticed Arden was cradled in a stranger's arms.

Jane fixed Luke with a cold stare. "And *who* are you, may I ask? And what are you doing with my niece?"

Luke swallowed his retort and glanced at Arden for help. She rolled her eyes, pushed his overcoat aside and scrambled to her feet. He smothered a groan and joined her.

"Hello, Aunt Jane, Uncle Arthur," Arden managed as she tried to straighten her disheveled appearance. Her velvet gown was limp and crushed beyond repair. She gave up the effort and turned her attention to her relatives. "I'm so glad to see you!" she lied.

"I doubt it, young lady." Arden's shirttail relative countered as she continued to glare at Luke. "Considering what's going on in front of my eyes, I'm sure I'm probably the last person you wanted to see!"

Her aunt didn't look the least bit intimidated by Luke's dark appearance and forbidding manner, Arden realized with a sinking feeling. Visions of her aunt's face if she caught a glimpse of the handcuff on his wrist or the chain leading to the briefcase flashed in front of her eyes. As her father's distant relative, Jane Peterson would no doubt report what she'd seen as soon as she could insert coins in the nearest pay telephone. And, if she were true to form, fiction would be greater than facts.

Her aunt's eyes glittered with suspicion and curiosity as she took in Arden and Luke. "Humph! In a public place! How could you? Have you forgotten you're the daughter of a respected minister?"

"Now, Aunt Jane, please don't leap to conclusions," Arden pleaded. "No matter what you think, things aren't what they seem to be."

Growing up, Arden had always been reminded she must be an example for the other children in the congregation, and told she should let her conscience be her guide. But she wasn't a child anymore, and her conscience seemed to be doing just fine.

She took a deep breath. "It's a long story, but if you'll give me a minute I'll tell you what happened."

"What is there to explain? The last I heard, you were going to be married to John Travers. That was only a few days ago. Now look at you." Jane pointedly eyed a sprig of mistletoe in Arden's hair and another in the vee of her wedding dress. Her accusing gaze took in the bottle of champagne at Arden's feet. "Where *is* John, anyway?"

"Home, I guess," Arden replied, beginning to seethe under her aunt's prying eyes.

Her aunt snorted. "You guess? How could you not know? Who is *this* man and what are you doing here in his arms?"

"This is Luke McCauley. Luke, meet my Aunt Jane and Uncle Arthur Peterson."

Luke smothered a groan when he noticed couples in the near vicinity had perked up and were listening to the conversation. On a scale of one to ten, his luck had sunk below zero. The only thing left to broadcast his identity to the whole terminal would have been a banner hung across the lounge with his name printed in scarlet letters. So far, he wasn't aware of anyone in the vicinity who didn't know his name. And, after the night's events, for sure they'd all remember him.

The more people who could identify him, the less chance he had to fade easily into the sunset tomorrow.

He had a score to settle with the Majestic Hotel owners, too, he thought darkly. The damn briefcase they insisted be chained to his wrist may have been an innocent precaution to them, but in the eyes of a beholder, a dead giveaway. As for getting involved with Arden's stolen luggage, that probably happened regularly around here. But he shouldn't have gotten involved.

He watched Arden's complexion turn white as her aunt continued with her harangue. His heart went out to Arden. He'd be damned if he'd let her take the flak for her innocent acceptance of his impulsive invitation to join him.

Luke quickly realized no excuse he could invent on the spur of the moment would improve matters for Arden, nor for himself, either. Not unless he made the ultimate sacrifice.

He took a deep breath and made an incredible decision.

He pulled Arden close to his side and under the guise of taking the mistletoe out of her hair, whispered in her ear. "Let me handle this. Okay?" She nodded.

"I'm Luke McCauley," he repeated, "Arden's husband."

"Husband?" Jane and Arthur were left with their mouths open.

"Actually," Luke continued, "I'm here on business—"

"Husband? Business? What kind of business?" Uncle Arthur hooted. "Never heard a honeymoon called business before."

"Combined with a honeymoon," Luke finished smoothly. "Your niece was decent enough to go along with me when I suggested we combine the two." He eyed Arthur Peterson blandly, daring him to say something else.

"I don't believe that for one minute, young man! Arden was supposed to marry John Travers this afternoon," Arden's aunt retorted. "Even the wedding invitations said so."

"I guess you might say my plans changed at the last minute," Arden managed. Her voice broke in a squeak when Luke threw his arm around her and pulled her close. The briefcase made a thud as it landed against her side. The chain rattled. Arden groaned.

Jane and Arthur Peterson's eyes bugged.

"True," Luke agreed, hurriedly putting the briefcase behind him. "Our marriage was kind of sudden...an elopement, if you will. Because of some urgent business I have waiting for me, we couldn't wait for a more formal ceremony."

"Who *are* you, young man?" Arthur Peterson demanded, "and what's on your wrist? Is that a handcuff?"

Luke shrugged. Arden's uncle turned on his niece. "Arden Crandall, does your father know what kind of man you married?"

"No, but I'm sure one of you is going to be first to tell him," Arden muttered under her breath. Her polite respect for the Petersons was strained. Enough was enough.

"Lord above, the man's a criminal!" Jane Peterson announced.

"No, Aunt Jane. Luke's a courier," Arden corrected. "Anyway, the thing with John began to fall apart before—'' Arden stopped when her aunt's lips tightened and her eyes narrowed. Suddenly Arden realized she didn't owe the Petersons anything. Not even the truth. They'd never accept the truth, anyway. Maybe because it wasn't lurid enough.

She had nothing to lose now. Arthur and Jane Peterson were related to her father only by marriage and, saint that her father was, he put up with them only out of some misguided sense of family loyalty. Anyone less charitable than he would have told them long ago to take their annoying ways and disappear.

Jane continued her harangue. "For shame, young lady! Your father isn't as young as he used to be. And for all you know, his heart might not be strong enough to take all of this."

Her father's heart! Arden froze. "What do you mean? What's wrong with my father's heart?"

"Nothing that I know of for certain," her aunt replied tartly. "But it wouldn't surprise me one bit if your behavior didn't give the poor man a heart attack!"

Arden's own heart leaped in her chest. "Luke, I have to find a telephone and call my father!"

"You haven't changed your mind about going on with the tour, have you?" he asked.

"No," Arden said worriedly as she dug into her purse. "I just want to make sure my father's all right! Drat, I don't have enough coins."

"It's a little late to worry about that, isn't it?" Arden's aunt remarked.

"No, Aunt Jane. It's never too late to do the right thing."

Her aunt rolled her eyes. "Let's hope so." She sniffed.

"Here, use this," Luke said as he offered Arden his telephone credit card. He whispered his identity number in her ear. "Take as long as you like. I'll wait right here for you."

He gazed somberly after Arden as she took off at a run for the nearest telephone. For some reason the thought bothered him that the telephone call might end her dream of independence after less than twenty-four hours of freedom. She deserved more of a chance than that.

"I'm going with Arden and talk to her father myself," her aunt Jane announced. "Maybe the two of us can talk some sense into her. I can't let her go through with this dreadful nonsense!"

Luke took her firmly by the shoulder. "I don't think so. There's nothing dreadful about this. Just a marriage between people who love each other. Why don't you wait right here with me? My wife won't be long."

Love, marriage, wife! How strange the words sounded to his ears. He'd joked about it off and on during the evening with Arden, but he was dead serious now. If it was the only way to keep the Petersons from spreading gossip about Arden, so be it.

"Dad? It's me, Arden."

"Thank the Lord," her father answered. "I've been praying you would call."

"Are you feeling okay?"

"Okay?" he thundered through the telephone. "How could I be feeling okay?"

"Is it your heart?" Arden held her breath waiting for his answer. If she'd been the cause of an impending heart attack, she would never forgive herself.

"My heart? What does my heart have to do with this!"

Maybe a lot more than he ever dreamed, she thought. If he were actually ill, she'd have to go home. "Aunt Jane told me your heart is weak."

"Aunt Jane? Jane Peterson? What were you doing with that old gossip? There's nothing between that woman's ears, and her tongue wags at both ends. My heart is fine. More to the point, it's you who concerns me."

"Don't worry about me, Dad. Now that I know Aunt Jane was wrong, I'm doing fine."

"Is that all you can say, young lady, you're fine?" her father thundered. "Don't you realize how you have humiliated me? No, don't say another word, just come home."

This was the first time Arden had ever really confronted her father or done anything he hadn't approved of. Not that she hadn't been tempted before, but she respected him too much to hurt him. This was something she'd had to do, or she would never be free of his loving restraints. Restraints that had almost led her to marry the wrong man.

"I never intended to humiliate you, Dad. I just realized marrying John was wrong. After all," she added as she forced laughter into her voice even as she choked back tears, "you and Mom taught me to recognize right from wrong. It just took me a little while to realize how wrong I was. I was afraid you wouldn't understand, so I left."

"It seems to me you haven't learned anything I taught you," her father thundered into the phone. "If you had, you never would have run away from your own wedding. I insist you come home right now. We can talk this over later."

Even though Arden could visualize her father's choleric, reddened face, she was determined not to give in. If she went home, he would be the one to do the talking, she would be the one who had to listen. It was now or never.

"I can't, Dad."

Arden heard her mother crying in the background. John's voice was asking to speak to her. She had to hang up before she allowed herself to be persuaded to go home. Somehow she had to make her father understand she had to live her own life.

"Dad, I love you, but I have to go. Please tell Mom not to worry and that I'll call later."

"Wait! Listen to me! I demand you come home immediately!"

"I'm sorry, I can't do that," Arden answered sadly. "I'm not your little girl anymore. Listening to you is what put me in this position in the first place. I have to see if I can make it on my own."

"Jezebel!"

"No, Dad. Just me, Arden. I'm sorry if I can't make you understand. I love you and Mom, but I have to do this. I have to be my own woman, not just your child. This is the only way I know to do it." She choked a little on the last words. "Goodbye."

Arden hurried back to find her aunt and uncle. It had been painful trying to explain to her father the enormous changes that were happening in her life. But it would be a pleasure to tell off Jane and Arthur.

She found Luke alone.

"What did you do with my aunt and uncle?"

"I persuaded them you were in good hands, namely mine. I also strongly suggested they leave." He looked off into the distance, grimaced. "That aunt of yours is some pistol. I somehow have the feeling you haven't heard the last of her."

"She's probably off somewhere calling my father right now."

"That shouldn't make a difference as long as you reached him before she does. You did, didn't you?"

"Yes," Arden answered mournfully. "For all the good it did me."

"Is he well?"

"Thank goodness, yes. Aunt Jane was mistaken about his health. But he's still too upset to be reasonable. In fact, I didn't get a chance to tell him much. I'm hoping he'll come around eventually."

"You can bet your aunt will pad the story from her imagination," Luke said dryly. "I just hope she doesn't mention the briefcase when she tells him about me. That would be enough to give the poor man a heart attack even if he hasn't a weak heart."

Arden shuddered. "I wish you could get rid of it. It gives me the willies."

"Me, too, for that matter. But I don't have a prayer of opening the lock. Not yet. Just what did your father have to say?"

"He told me I'm going to go to hell!" Arden said the words defiantly, but there was obviously still some pain. After all, he *was* her father.

"He doesn't really mean it, I'm sure," Luke said. "But even so, I guess you'd have plenty of company," he laughed. "Me included. Did you tell him we were married?"

"No, should I have?"

There was a pause while Luke considered the question.

"Probably, if you didn't want him to worry. But that's okay. I'm sure your Aunt Jane will get around to telling him for you. And with my luck, there'll be an all-points bulletin out for a Luke McCauley any time now. Come on, let's see if we can get lost in the crowd."

There, he'd made a commitment in spite of himself. But how could he not have when Arden needed him?

"Paging Miss Arden Crandall. Please pick up the courtesy telephone at your gate."

"Oh, no, it must be my father," Arden said. She looked around her wildly. "He's found out where I am!"

"Did you tell him you were here?" Luke asked.

"No. But I'll bet Aunt Jane did." Anxiously Arden hurried to pick up the red courtesy telephone.

"Arden? This is your father. Jane just called. She tells me you claim to be married!"

Arden thought fast. How should she answer? She'd never lied to her father and she wouldn't start now.

"Sort of, but that's not the whole story."

"Sort of?" he snorted. "And to a man like the one you're with? Either you are or you aren't!"

"What did Aunt Jane tell you about Luke?"

"When I got that woman calmed down, she told me some fool story about a man with a handcuff on his wrist. She told me he's a criminal!"

"He's not a criminal, Dad. Far from it. He's a wonderful man who's taken good care of me. As for the handcuff, he's a courier delivering a briefcase."

"It still doesn't sound to me as if he's very trustworthy. How could you marry someone like that just minutes after you abandoned a fine man like John?"

Arden heard the genuine pain in her father's voice and wished she could be there beside him. It would have made this conversation so much easier.

"I tried to explain it to Aunt Jane, but she wouldn't listen. She was set on believing the worst. Luke isn't..."

Luke reached over her shoulder and took the phone with his free hand. He drew Arden close to him with the other.

"This is Luke McCauley, sir. I just want to tell you Arden is fine and that she's in good hands." He held the phone away from his ear when there was shouting on the other end.

"No, sir," Luke returned quietly. "There hasn't been any sin. You have my word on it."

"The word of a criminal!"

"No, Mr. Crandall. I assure you I'm not a criminal. I'm sorry you feel that way. And I'm sorry for Arden, too. She's a fine woman and she deserves respect and understanding."

Luke felt a pang of guilt. It was true he'd contemplated disappearing with the contents of the briefcase. He hadn't quite made up his mind. Was it because he hadn't had the chance? Or was it because he knew he wasn't actually a thief at heart?

There was a long silence from the other end. "Let me talk to my daughter."

Luke shrugged and handed the phone back to Arden.

"Daughter, stay where you are. I'll come to get you."

"No, it's impossible with this storm. I love you, Dad, but I'm on my own now. Yes, I know what I'm doing. Maybe someday you'll understand. Give my love to Mom. Goodbye."

There were tears in her eyes when she hung up. Luke held her to him and let her tears flow against his chest. He knew from experience how hard it was to make the decision to forge a new life. How much harder would it be for a woman like Arden?

"You'll be fine, Arden," he told her. "It's just going to take some time. Cutting loose from the past isn't easy, but I'd say you just took a giant step."

Chapter Four

"Hey!" a happy bridegroom hollered, holding up a bottle of champagne just as Arden and Luke returned to the gate area. "As long as we're stuck here for the duration, why don't we have ourselves a wedding reception?"

"A wedding reception? In an airport terminal?" someone in the background asked.

"Why not?" a woman answered. "We might as well. It looks as if we're going to miss the one Majestic planned for us at their hotel."

"Good idea," another groom announced. "Sweetheart, where did you put the bottle of champagne Majestic gave us that we were saving for later?"

"Turn up the radio. Maybe there's music for dancing."

"Hey, I've got my guitar!"

"And I've got my harmonica!"

"Casey, are you sure we can have our wedding reception right here?"

"Why not?" the man called Casey answered. "It looks as if it's going to be the only reception we're going to have tonight."

"You're right!" Agnes Chambers, the tour leader, agreed. "Here, have another bottle of champagne. I've given out one to each party, but I seem to have one left."

The babel of voices grew louder as honeymooners fell into the spirit of the spontaneous party. Someone turned up the volume on a portable radio. Christmas carols filled the air. The inconvenience of the winter storm that delayed the tour's departure was forgotten.

A happy groom thrust an open bottle of champagne at Luke. "Here, have a drink!"

"No, thanks, later maybe," Luke smiled halfheartedly as he headed for a quieter spot. At the rate things were going, he didn't stand a prayer of fading into the background. But his plans hadn't changed. He was going to stay out of sight, and come hell or high water, tomorrow was going to be the start of his new life.

"Hey, wait a minute! Is it legal to carry liquor in the terminal?" someone questioned.

"Carry it, yes," a voice answered. "But I heard you can only drink liquor at bars. But what the hell, who's going to care?"

Luke glanced at the commotion surrounding them. "The guy's right," he told Arden. "Legal or not, I don't think anyone's going to be able to stop the party. Not tonight. Airport Security is bound to be too busy with bigger problems tonight to bother with something like this."

He winced at a particularly loud shout in his ear. "With the way my luck is going tonight, I'd be the one to go to jail if I so much as lifted a glass with liquor in it."

"Can we dance, too?" Arden asked wistfully as the music started and several couples started to dance. She cradled a bottle of champagne someone had given her and looked up into his wary dark eyes. "It might help pass the time. Anyway, I hear it's relaxing."

Relax when he was surrounded by any number of law officers waiting for him to take a misstep? Or an ex-con or two trying to get even with him? How little this woman knew about him! And, as far as he was concerned, he intended to keep it that way.

On the other hand, there *was* Arden to consider. She'd been through a lot and deserved any respite the night could bring.

He gazed down at her. "Are you sure you want to dance?" he asked, waving back a happy party goer and a fresh shower of mistletoe.

"Yes. I'm just trying to fit in with the crowd," she answered. "We *are* supposed to be honeymooners, aren't we?"

Luke shook off another celebrant before he turned back to Arden. "Just don't get carried away, Mrs. McCauley, this isn't real," he said, glancing at the wistful expression on her face. "We're only going to be married long enough to get you to Cancún. Anyway," he added, looking around at the tour group couples who were getting deeper into the spirit of the party, "I don't think you'll want me to ask you to dance if you stop to think about it."

Arden took two seconds to decide there was nothing to think about. Margo had secretly taught her to dance, and she'd dreamed of dancing with a man like Luke for a long time. "Why not?"

"The briefcase will get in our way," he explained. "And that bottle of champagne isn't going to help, either."

"I'll manage," Arden answered as the strains of "I'll be Home for Christmas" filled the air. "If we don't get into the spirit of things, everyone will wonder why. You don't want that to happen, do you?" she asked in a tone that touched and surprised him.

"Arden," he said, as he shook the briefcase so the chain rattled, "if I take you in my arms, I'll have this damn thing bouncing against your backside." He took a quick look over her shoulder at the clinging contour of her wedding dress and flushed. "Besides, the briefcase will be right out in the open for everyone to see. They're bound to wonder what's in it and what I'm doing with it. As for you, you'll probably wind up more black-and-blue than ever."

"I don't mind. Colors fade. And, anyway, no one's going to see the bruises but me," Arden insisted, raising her arms to Luke, bottle and all. "If I don't mind, neither should you. I'm sure everyone is too busy dancing to pay attention to us."

"Okay," he reluctantly agreed. He wasn't going to bet on anyone *not* watching him, not after he'd already been questioned and probably would be again before the night was through.

He took in the growing revelry. If anyone in the tour group had noticed the briefcase, they were either too polite to comment on it or they were lost in a dream world of their own making.

"But I suggest you draw the line at drinking," he added, pointedly glancing at the bottle of champagne.

"From what you've told me about never having tasted liquor before, heaven only knows what you'd want to do if you started now."

"Oh, I've actually tasted liquor before. Margo saw to that. I just haven't done it often. For now, I just want to dance," Arden said, moving dreamily in time to the music.

"Say, you haven't been at the champagne already, have you?" Luke peered into her eyes. "Somehow, this doesn't seem like you."

"That's the whole idea," she agreed. "I'm not the old Arden Crandall anymore. That girl would never think of drinking and dancing in public."

"Never?"

"Never. Not that I haven't wanted to. But wanting and doing are two different things," she added before she grinned happily. "Thank goodness those days are behind me. As for my having some champagne, I just might do that too, later."

"Not if I can help it," Luke muttered. "You'll have to settle for a dance."

It was becoming clear to him that the only way to satisfy the new Arden was to give in to the little things that meant a lot to her.

As "I'll be Home for Christmas" tinkled out of the radio, he noticed the tears that appeared at the corners of Arden's expressive eyes. She might be determined to start a new life, but memories of her old one were still obviously fresh.

Touched, he took her in his arms. He carefully settled the briefcase in the small of her back and slowly circled a two-by-four-inch square of the cement terminal floor in time to the music.

"So, tell me, how do you like the road to independence so far?" he asked to distract her, and himself, too. He was trying not to react to the way her nearness was affecting him. In spite of his determination to remain detached, his feelings for her were getting stronger. Thank God it was happening in an airport terminal surrounded by hundreds of strangers where he couldn't do a damn thing about it.

"I like it fine," Arden responded, her head nestled in Luke's shoulder, her left hand clutched in his right. "The nicest part of it is that it's only just begun."

Luke felt a momentary sense of alarm. Was she referring to herself? Or did she think something permanent was possible between the two of them? No woman had been able to claim him as her own, and none ever would if he had anything to say about it. Still, it was becoming more and more difficult to ignore the slender, supple figure swaying so seductively in his arms.

Arden felt Luke's warmth envelope her. How could she have ever thought she was cold? she wondered as she nestled closer. When his arms tightened around her, she murmured her pleasure. Being held in the embrace of this unknown, dark and perhaps dangerous man was her fantasy come to life.

Except, she reminded herself, it *was* only fantasy. She couldn't let herself get carried away on her first night of freedom and by the first man she'd become attracted to. There was still a lot of living to do ahead of her.

She tried to ignore the briefcase swaying gently against her back. It was just a minor annoyance, she thought dreamily. Well worth a bruise or two to be held so close by the man who'd walked out of her dreams.

He might be a man she'd met for the first time tonight. A man who, in her fantasy, was danger and mystery personified. He might be a man she'd wished into existence, but his solid strength was real.

He was also a man to whom she would say goodbye tomorrow. But, she thought with a smile, he was hers for now. And from the way he was holding her and lightly caressing the small of her back, he didn't seem at all unhappy about dancing with her, after all.

The song on the radio changed to "White Christmas." In the background, a lone guitarist delicately provided an accompaniment to voices softly singing the song that had become Christmas in everyone's mind.

Briefly meeting Luke's eyes, she could see he was deep in thought. Maybe he was remembering another white Christmas with someone he loved. Not a wife, surely. He didn't seem to be the kind to be married and to have a family. Yet, what did she really know about him? So far he'd revealed very little of himself to her.

He appeared to be a man who was a loner, a man of mystery who kept his affairs to himself. A man not afraid of facing danger. But there was a look in his eye that told her he still had vulnerable human qualities and a capacity for tenderness.

Maybe that was the combination that drew her.

"Merry Christmas!" a reveler shouted as he threw sprigs of mistletoe into the air.

Luke caught a sprig and held it over Arden's head. His gaze locked with hers. "Merry Christmas."

He lowered his lips to hers. Before she could react, he kissed her. With a gentle pressure he kissed the lips that had fascinated him so, until he heard a small sigh of pleasure.

She was lost in the taste of his lips, the raspy feel of his unshaven skin as it brushed against her cheek, the male scent of him as he pulled her against him. Sensations she'd never experienced before shot through her and almost took her breath away. His strong arms, his kiss, his warm breath on her brow made her feel more wanted, safe, more cared for than she'd ever been in her adult life. And more like a desirable woman.

Suddenly she was grateful for the ice and snow that had kept them in the airport terminal; and grateful she'd listened to her heart instead of her head when she'd taken the chance and accepted his invitation to join him.

The sound of the dreamy, nostalgic Christmas music sent her thoughts wandering down sensuous paths Margo had hinted at and that she'd never dared to dwell on before. With a sigh of contentment, she nestled deeper into the hard, masculine arms that held her as if they would never let her go.

Luke cleared his throat at the sigh. Pretend wife or no, mistletoe or no, he had allowed Arden to come too close for comfort. It wasn't fair to her, not when it had only been an impulse on his part that had brought her into his arms in the first place. An impulse he was bound to regret if he let the attraction between them mess up his clear thinking.

It wasn't fair to her to hold her so close for another reason. This time more for her sake than his. There were angry men out there who had sworn to get even with him. And not even having Arden in his arms would stop them.

"Merry Christmas," Luke repeated softly, before he reluctantly pulled away. He stood there for a long moment gazing down into her shining eyes and soft smile. This Arden Crandall was getting into his blood too soon and too fast. And for the life of him, he couldn't seem to put the brakes on it. "Come on," he said with a sigh, "let's find a place to relax for a while."

The last thing he needed was to start thinking of the woman in his arms as the wife in his arms.

Listening to his heart instead of listening to his head was becoming dangerous. At the rate he and Arden kept celebrating Christmas, kissing under mistletoe and giving in to the sounds and the mood of the season, he'd soon be in deep trouble for sure. If he kept this up, he'd probably wind up delivering precious cargo for someone else for another ten years instead of living high off the hog himself. If he didn't wind up dead first.

"That's about enough," he said abruptly. Without waiting for her reply, he abruptly lowered his arms and made for the corner he and Arden had occupied. He'd worked too hard and waited too long for a lucky break to soften now. As intriguing as she might be, he wasn't going to let Arden Crandall mess things up for him.

Bewildered by another of Luke's abrupt mood changes, Arden struggled to pull herself together. She wasn't sure of the paths her thoughts had been taking her, but one thing was clear: she'd better remember the husband-and-wife bit wasn't real. She gazed after Luke, dark, handsome and mysterious. With an unintentional charisma that drew her in spite of herself. Maybe it was a good thing she *would* see the last of him tomorrow, she thought wistfully as she followed him to where they'd found each other.

"Damn," Luke exclaimed, when he saw the empty space they'd left behind. "Will you look at that!"

"Look at what?" Arden asked looking around her. "I don't see anything."

"That's the point. First, it was your luggage, now it's mine! Someone's made off with my overnight bag, and unless you gave it to someone to hold, your raincoat's gone, too."

Arden blinked, her dreamy mood shattered. Reality set in. Sure enough, the spot where they'd been sitting was empty. Luggage thieves had been busy while they'd been dancing.

She felt ashamed of the brief moments earlier that night when she'd first thought Luke might be an accomplice of the luggage thieves. Or maybe something even worse. Of course, she hadn't actually believed he wasn't on the up-and-up, she told herself, or she would never have joined him.

More to the point, she realized, as she studied an angry Luke, any brief suspicions she might have had about him had very little to do with the way she felt about him. She'd been so attracted to him she'd thrown caution to the winds, even though she'd known she was taking a chance.

"I don't suppose I'll need my raincoat where I'm going," she finally answered. "As for your overnight bag, maybe you won't need it, either," she told him, trying to comfort him. "You did say you intended to go right back to New York on the return flight, didn't you?"

He cast her a sharp look but didn't answer.

"You folks have to stop using liquor on city property," a stern voice spoke up over the sound of "Jingle Bells." "It's okay to party, but not if you're drinking. There's a law about having open bottles of booze in an airport terminal."

Luke swung around to meet the sharp gaze of the same security officer who had earlier taken the report about Arden's luggage. His heartbeat stepped up its pace. This guy was one of the last people he wanted to meet again.

"Officer, you're just in time!" Arden told the guard eagerly. "My husband has just had his luggage stolen, too!"

"Husband? Are you sure about that?" The guard's gaze swung from Arden's bare wedding ring finger and back to Luke.

"Er…yes, he is," Arden answered. A cold wave of apprehension swept over her. Why had she called Luke her husband? Why had she drawn more attention to them even after Luke had reminded her that attention was the last thing he wanted.

"Well, I don't mind telling you that back a couple of hours ago it didn't sound as if he was your husband. In fact, if I remember correctly, I heard you tell him to mind his own business!"

"That was just a lover's quarrel," Luke broke in. "My wife tends to overreact in moments of stress, don't you, dear?" He gathered Arden under his arm. The briefcase hanging from his wrist swung right into Arden's middle with a whooshing sound.

She caught her breath, steadied the briefcase against her stomach and gave Luke a tight smile.

"Some honeymoon you two are having," the guard commented dryly. "With both of you already fighting and that briefcase getting in the way, I wouldn't want to bet on how long your marriage is going to last!"

"Long enough," Luke answered. He gave Arden a warning squeeze.

He should have known better than to accept the cockamamie briefcase delivery job that branded him an untrustworthy character. Just as he should have known better than to hook up with Arden. He'd been too weak to pass up either temptation.

"Want to make a report?" the guard asked.

In a growing list of possible ways to identify him and connect him and the briefcase in everyone's mind, the last thing Luke wanted now was to file a report. Especially since he knew that his name and description were probably already being investigated right now because of the gun he'd declared.

"Truthfully, I didn't have many things of value in the bag," Luke explained. "Shaving gear, a change of underwear and a fresh shirt." When the guard's brow rose in a question, Luke hurried to add, "And a couple pairs of swimming trunks. Considering where we were going, I was traveling light."

"I'll say," the guard said skeptically. "Somehow, I don't envy you two one bit. You're sure you don't want to file a report?"

"Yeah, I'm sure. Don't worry about it. I'll do fine. In fact," Luke said as he glanced at Arden, "this will give us a reason to do some shopping in Cancún. I'm sure my wife is looking forward to it."

He'd intended to discard his suit, overcoat, gloves and scarf at the earliest opportunity, anyway, and take on a new identity, clothing included. Where he planned on going, the sun would always shine, the moon would set on crystal-clear waters, and English wouldn't be the language of choice. But, he thought fiercely, it definitely wasn't going to be anywhere south of the border where Arden might be. She spelled trouble with a capital *T*.

"Okay, if you say so. But remember, all of you," the security guard's voice rose to a crescendo as he pointedly looked at the bottle of champagne clutched in Arden's hand, "No more drinking on airport property unless it's in a bar!"

Luke waited until the guard was out of sight.

"Come on, we've got some shopping to do!"

"I thought we were going to shop in Cancún," Arden answered, puzzled at another of Luke's mercurial mood changes. "I'm not sure any of the gift shops are open this late."

"Take it from me," he said dryly, urging her along. "No concession is going to close when there are thousands of captive shoppers around. And especially since most of us have nothing else to do.''

"Okay," Arden agreed, stepping up her pace. "But what kind of shopping did you have in mind?"

"You'll see," he answered, glancing into well-lit gift shops. At the third shop, he came to a stop in front of a vending machine. "This one ought to do."

"Do for what?" Arden peered at the huge plastic bubble. It was full of small, plastic oval containers, some with miniature toys inside, others with candy or bubble gum. The machine was a child's diversion and certainly nothing she could imagine Luke wanting or needing.

"You call this shopping?"

"Yeah," he answered digging into his trouser pockets. "Damn! Got a couple of quarters?"

Arden opened her purse, extracted her coin purse and handed him the coins. "You don't really intend to put the money in there, do you?"

"You bet!" Luke inserted the quarters, turned the crank and out fell a small container. Inside was a square of bubble gum. "Two more quarters, please." He scowled at the plastic bubble as he held out his hand.

"You got your bubble gum, aren't you satisfied?" Arden gave him two more quarters.

"I don't chew gum," he said absently as he studied the machine. "Here, you can have it."

"No, thanks," Arden answered. "And furthermore," she said, as she rummaged in the bottom of her purse for change and thrust it out to him, "these are the last of my quarters. From now on, you'll have to find your own.''

''Not when I have what I was looking for!'' Luke held up the plastic bubble to the light. ''Hold still for a minute,'' he said as he twisted the container open and extracted the one-size-fits-all ring. ''Give me your left hand.''

Mesmerized by the sheer quirkiness of the situation, Arden stuck out her hand.

Luke tried to slip the plain gold band on her ring finger and silently muttered his frustration when it didn't fit. He adjusted the ring to make it bigger and tried again.

''There,'' he announced with satisfaction, holding her hand up to the light. ''Now no one's going to question whether we're married.''

Arden stared at the ersatz wedding ring for a moment then back at Luke. ''You call this a wedding ring?'' She looked inside the shop. Her glance lingered on a display of jewelry. ''I can understand why you felt you had to buy me a ring, but was this the best you could think of?''

''Without attracting attention, yes,'' Luke remarked impatiently. ''It would have looked suspicious to anyone watching if I bought you a real wedding ring in there after everyone thinks we're already married.''

''You may be right,'' she answered. ''But it seems to me no woman should have to pay for her own wedding ring! Even if it only cost one dollar.''

Luke sighed and handed her a five dollar bill. ''Keep the change. Anything else?''

''Yes,'' she answered firmly, determined to keep the

situation light even though her heart was waltzing to three-quarter time around her chest at the thought of being Luke's wife. "Just keep in mind, putting a wedding ring on my finger doesn't actually make me your wife!"

"Relax," Luke answered. "How many times do I have to remind you this is all an act, for your sake as well as mine?"

"I grant you it started out that way, but we seem to be getting in deeper and deeper."

"Arden, I swear to you the ring's only for cover. The way the guard kept glancing at your finger, I knew I had to do something fast."

Arden eyed the gold ring. The metal seemed to shine under the red-and-green glass Christmas globe revolving above her head. The ring might have cost only one dollar, but it somehow seemed more real than the genuine gold wedding rings in the glass case inside the shop. And very precious. Perhaps it was because the ring was part of her fantasy and because Luke had given it to her. "I just hope it doesn't turn my finger green," she commented softly, holding her hand up to the light.

"In the space of a few hours? Hardly likely," Luke answered, glancing around them. "You can take it off as soon as we get to Cancún. Come on, let's go back. The guard's not in sight."

If Luke only knew. It was a ring Arden intended to keep forever.

"Well," she conceded, keeping her thoughts to herself, "I'll wear the ring to keep us both out of trouble. That *is* why you gave it to me, isn't it?"

Luke swallowed his answer. Sure it had been part of a charade. But putting it on her finger had left him with a strange feeling, almost as if she were his bride. A feeling he wasn't too sure was good for him.

Chapter Five

Arden discovered how wrong she could be when the lights in the terminal clicked off and on again. A sure sign there was an important announcement coming. In minutes, to loud groans, the bad news came over the loud speakers.

"Attention. Your attention, please. In response to the many inquiries about departing flights, we now have official confirmation that no flights will be allowed in or out of JFK until at least eight o'clock tomorrow morning. Due to the lack of sufficient machinery to clear the runways and the continuing storm, it is possible there will be further postponements. The City of New York regrets any inconvenience this delay has caused."

An instant clamor broke out at the neighboring gate. Shouting their dismay, angry passengers ran up to the check-in counter. Children cried.

"*Non, non,* I must return home at once!"

"My ticket is for tonight!" another passenger insisted. "I demand to be flown to Paris immediately! I cannot wait until morning!"

"I'm sorry, sir. No flights have been authorized for

departure until morning,'' the counter agent protested as the crowd around her grew more and more agitated. ''Besides, the flight crew was sent home hours ago.''

''Then I demand you order them to return!'' a tall man with a scarf tied over his head and under his chin to keep warm shouted. ''It is freezing in here!'' He shook his clenched fist under the startled attendant's nose.

Another irate passenger shook his clenched fist under the agent's nose. ''My family is waiting for me at De Gaulle! They will wonder what has happened to me!''

''Don't worry about that, sir. The authorities at De Gaulle and all other airports throughout the world have been notified of the delay. There's nothing I can do for you. Except to put you all on standby for the first available flights.''

''Standby? Are you saying there is no guarantee I will have a seat on the next plane?'' he shouted. He waved his ticket under her nose. ''I will not put up with such a delay. I must get on the plane!''

''We'll do our best,'' the agent replied, clearly dismayed. She took a tentative step backward when the crowd surged toward her. Angry voices rose to a crescendo.

The horde of passengers milling around the agent became more and more unruly. Several looked ready to jump over the counter. The agent looked more and more apprehensive and threw up her hands as if to defend herself.

Luke started forward. ''Wait here,'' he told Arden. ''I'm going over there to see if I can help. It looks as if that man's about to jump over the counter and attack that poor woman!''

"Luke, wait!" Arden grabbed his sleeve. "What if real trouble starts and you get involved? You'll only be drawing more attention to yourself!"

Luke paused in midstride. Arden was right. More attention was the last thing he needed.

The beleaguered agent reached under the counter. An alarm sounded, a red light started to blink over her head. Security guards made for melee.

"Good Lord!" Their tour leader glanced around her own group apprehensively. She reached for her cellular phone and spoke for a few minutes. "I was told the latest announcement was intended to forestall any further problems. Instead, it looks as if it backfired, doesn't it?"

"What's the matter? Wasn't *no* good enough for those people?" Luke inquired.

"Evidently not." The tour leader laughed uneasily. "It's a good thing you people are taking the delay so well!"

Taking things so well?

Luke didn't look so agreeable to Arden. But everything was okay with her. The night was rapidly turning into an adventure, thanks to Luke.

"By the way," Agnes Chambers announced, "I'd like to take this opportunity while we're all together to check you all against my passenger list. In all the excitement, and the way you all kept moving around, I couldn't do it until now. But it is important. When I call your names, please answer 'here,' just as if we're back in school." She smiled at the broad groans at her remark.

"Adams, Alcott," she called out, checking names off the list as the couples made themselves known. "Border, Delancy, McCauley, Morgan…" Her voice droned on and on as she read through the alphabetical listing and listened for the affirmative replies. "Travers?" There was no reply. "Is there a Mr. and Mrs. John Travers here?"

Arden glanced over at Luke. He shrugged his shoulders.

The tour leader frowned, put a question mark next to the name and went on to finish the list.

"Maybe I should have answered when she called 'Travers'?" Arden whispered to Luke. "She's going to see my tour documents sooner or later."

"Just as well that you didn't," Luke replied dryly. "After all, I'd already answered to McCauley. Since we're together, it was bound to raise some questions."

"Well, I guess there's no harm done. At least until we board the plane," Arden said worriedly. "We'll just have to think of some diversion if we're discovered."

"Let's cross that bridge when the time comes," Luke answered. "Until then, I have other troubles to worry about."

"Troubles? What kind of troubles?"

"The guy standing over there on your left is checking me over," he muttered under his breath.

"Who?" Arden gazed around her. There were a dozen people in her view. Until someone shifted and she saw a familiar face. "You mean the security guard?"

"Right. The one who helped me chase the Smiths after your luggage was stolen. And the one you told about my lost luggage. No, don't stare at him," he whispered urgently. "Damn, he's coming over. Now remember, you're my wife and we were married yesterday!"

"How could I forget?" Arden answered, nervously twisting the bubble-gum-machine wedding ring.

The guard came to a stop in front of Luke. He held a small poster in his hand.

"After I talked to you, something about the two of you kept bugging me. So I stopped in the security office and found this." He shoved a Man-Wanted poster at Luke. "Mind answering a few questions?" he asked.

"Not at all." Luke replied amiably. "What's up?"

The officer checked Luke's appearance against the poster, quietly reading aloud the vital statistics of the wanted criminal.

"Height, six feet three inches. Weight, one hundred and eighty-five pounds. Hair, eyes, brown." His voice trailed off. "Except for the mustache, the description sure fits you. Darn near one hundred percent. It doesn't say anything about that scar on your chin, but I guess you could have gotten that after this picture was taken." Frowning, he turned to Arden.

"You sure this man is your husband?"

"Why, yes," Arden replied sweetly. "What makes you think he's not?"

Luke looked on in silent approval. Hell, he was used

to being questioned. But Arden? With her background, she must have more than a few reservations about the situation. Instead, she was quick on the uptake and with her answers. Seeing her wide-eyed, innocent expression, he knew he hadn't given her enough credit. She was a damn good actress.

"Because your husband resembles a wanted criminal, that's why," the suspicious guard replied. "Here, take a look at this and tell me if it isn't a match!"

He held up the poster for her to view. Sure enough, although the picture was grainy, Arden could see there was the same sable hair, square jaw and piercing eyes that had attracted her in the first place. Except that the eyes of the man in the poster looked cold, threatening. Luke's eyes as he quietly gazed at her now were enigmatic, but she knew they were capable of warmth.

Still, after one long look, Arden's heart sank. Except for the wanted man's mustache and the scar on Luke's chin, they looked enough alike to be brothers. But, on second thought, the man definitely wasn't as handsome, nor did he have that attractive mysterious edge surrounding Luke that appealed to her senses. Luke's glance sent shivers of excitement through her. The criminal's cold and deadly eyes sent shivers of fear.

But the Wanted poster did serve to remind her she didn't know all that much about Luke McCauley.

"There may be a slight resemblance, but I can assure you this man definitely isn't Luke," Arden announced after pretending to scrutinize the poster. Deciding to take the chance on Luke being the man he said he was, she pulled her thoughts together. "Except they do have the same hair coloring," she conceded.

"On the other hand, with this grainy print it may not be the same. What is this man wanted for?"

"Well, ma'am," the officer said with a sharp glance at Luke, "to start with, armed robbery."

Arden swallowed hard.

"Not only that," the guard said eyeing her narrowly, "I heard the guy had a female accomplice. From the description that came over the fax, she kind of sounds like you. Even to the blond hair."

"Sounds like me! Good heavens," Arden echoed. She kept her smile, but her blood ran cold. "Imagine that! And what does this woman have to do with the robbery?"

"She manned, er, drove the getaway car."

"It wasn't me," Arden answered firmly. "I was at home in Queens every day last week getting ready for my wedding. I can give you my home address and you can check if you want to." She prayed the guard wouldn't take her up on her offer.

For a minute the man looked as if he was going to. "No, thanks. I guess I'll pass for now." He pocketed the poster and turned back to Luke. "Where were you last week?"

"I couldn't have committed the crime. I was in Rio on business."

"Got anything to prove it?"

"Sure, but only if I have to," Luke answered. He returned the officer's piercing gaze with a noncommittal one of his own.

"Let's just say I'm asking. For now."

The man's voice held a veiled threat and a promise of things to come that Luke didn't care for.

He dug into his inside coat pocket and fished out his passport. As he handed it to the guard, he realized if he was smart, he'd better find a country to go to that didn't have an extradition agreement with the United States.

The suspicious guard leafed through Luke's passport. "Hong Kong, Sydney, Taipei, Guatemala, Manila, Rio... Sure get around don't you?"

"It's all in a day's work," Luke replied modestly. "I plan to give it all up after this commission."

"I guess you might be clean at that," the man remarked before he returned the passport. "At least for the bank robbery. But you have to admit the resemblance was close."

"Maybe to you, but not to me," Arden interjected. She mustered a dazzling smile. "I know you're doing your best. As you always do, I'm sure. Besides, Officer Hayden," she said as she took in the name tag on his uniform, "my husband has proved he wasn't in the country when the crime was committed. He's as innocent as I am. You don't suppose for one minute that *I* would have married him if he'd been a criminal, do you?"

To Luke, Arden looked soft and innocent.

The poor guard looked as if he ought to apologize.

Luke decided he couldn't have chosen a better champion if he'd tried.

What was he so worried about, anyway? Luke wondered, as the security guard continued to study him. So what if he did resemble the guy in the poster? He had an airtight alibi. But it was definitely something to be aware of in case someone else picked up on the resemblance.

Hell, it wasn't as if he'd done anything illegal. Not yet, anyway. With his background of working for the secret service, and thirty-two years of clean living, no one would think he was even considering it. Thinking about committing a crime wasn't in the same class as doing it, anyway. So, unless the lawman was a mind reader, which he doubted, as they exchanged stares, he was home free.

"Sorry if I worried you and your husband for nothing," the guard said, with a last, lingering look at Luke. "Just doing my job. I guess tonight is a heck of a way to start a honeymoon."

"You're right on both counts, of course," Luke answered with a smile that barely reached his lips.

"Of course," Arden echoed.

As soon as the man disappeared, Luke let out a big sigh. "I don't know why it had to be me again. There must be dozens of more suspicious characters running around the terminal tonight."

"If you don't mind my saying so, I would say it's the handcuff around your wrist," Arden commented dryly. "If I were you, I'd try to get rid of it any way you can. It's not doing either of us any good."

She'd come to Luke's defense not only for his sake, but for her own. After the officer had told her the bank robber had a blond female accomplice, the last thing she wanted was to start her new life with a night in jail while they checked her out. As for Luke, in spite of his assurances that he wasn't involved in the current crime, she couldn't be sure he had always been on the up-and-up.

The dark edge she'd sensed the first time she'd laid eyes on him had briefly returned when the guard had started to question them, but it was carefully hidden now.

Still, she was impressed by his confident demeanor and the way he'd handled the crisis. He appeared to be as worldly as she had been sheltered, and had probably seen a side of life and done things she could only dream about. It was too bad he wasn't going to be around long enough to be her tour guide on her own road to adventure.

"I could use a good stiff drink," Luke announced, still feeling the hot breath of the law breathing down his neck.

"I don't blame you," Arden agreed. "But before you do, I would like to ask you a couple of questions of my own."

"Shoot." From the frown on her forehead, he knew as sure as he knew his own name that Arden wasn't convinced he was an innocent man.

"*Are* you a wanted man?"

"No, ma'am." *Not yet, anyway.*

"*Have* you ever done anything the authorities could want you for?"

"No, never," he assured her with a straight face. That wasn't strictly true, either. It depended on which country and which authorities she was talking about.

"I've never even gotten a traffic ticket," he went on. "For that matter, I don't even own a car. I'm on the road too much to be bothered with one."

"You're positive?"

"I'm positive. You'll have to take me at my word," he said solemnly. "And for your information, I'm not the guy in the wanted photograph, either."

"You're willing to swear to all that?"

"I swear," Luke answered, raising his unencumbered right hand. "Why are you so concerned? You'll never see me again after tomorrow."

"I just wanted to make sure," Arden answered, looking down at the fake wedding ring. "After all, even though I hardly know you, I *have* told people I'm your wife." She wrapped her arms around herself, shivering as someone opened a service door and a blast of cold blew snow and ice inside.

"What's there to know?" Luke answered. If he told her the truth, he'd probably wind up alone. Gazing at her earnest expression, somehow he wasn't ready for that to happen. Not yet. But he owed her some kind of answer. "I'm just a guy trying to earn a living."

"Married?" she ventured.

"Yeah, to you," Luke said, mentally counting to ten. Before she was through, she'd probably want to know his birthday, how much he'd weighed at birth and if he had his own teeth. "Sorry, I'm not very exciting."

The expression on her face and the look in her eyes told him she thought otherwise. The poor soul actually thought he was exciting.

"Perhaps," she answered. "But you have to admit things *have* been a little unusual tonight."

Unusual! Luke shook his head. Only someone as unsophisticated as Arden would call the night's events "a little unusual." A more worldly woman would have turned and run for her life by now.

"Come on, Mrs. McCauley, let's go and get warm. I'd offer you my coat, but I can't get it off with this blasted thing chained to my wrist. Maybe if we stay put and mind our own business, everyone will forget we're here."

No sooner were they settled between two other weary couples, than there was another interruption.

"Sorry, folks, you'll have to move while we clean up this section."

Luke snapped to attention. A burly maintenance man with a trash barrel on wheels and an industrial vacuum at his side stood contemplating them. It took a second warning before someone turned off the radio. Luke could hear disgruntled growls at the man's announcement, even muttered threats. Considering all he'd been through tonight, he was tempted to add a few of his own.

"What do you mean, you have to clean this section? Take a look around you. In the first place, the airport's crowded. In the second place, it doesn't look as if there's any other place to go to that's not already full of people."

"Sorry. Just doing my job. I always start cleaning up after the last flight's gone. You folks can come back when I'm through if you want."

"The last flight hasn't gone anywhere, or hadn't you heard?" Luke asked, disgusted at the new turn of events. If he could have foreseen the way this last job of his was going to turn out, he might have refused it.

On the other hand, it presented a one-in-a-million opportunity. He couldn't have passed it up.

The maintenance man crossed his arms and shrugged.

Luke put a lid on his temper.

"Sorry, Arden, it looks as if we have to vacate the premises for a while."

"You don't suppose we could find something to eat? I've just realized how hungry I am."

"I doubt it. The food concessions are closed by now."

"Some of the gift shops are still open," the maintenance man offered. "My wife always says that when there's nothing else to do, it's time to go shopping."

"We've already gone shopping," Arden remarked, frowning down at her ring finger.

"That's okay," Luke said hurriedly before she could add anything else. "We can do it again."

"A few of the portable bars are open," the janitor said. "I heard there's some beer left in that one over there." He motioned to a bar about fifty feet away. "Better hurry, it can't last much longer."

"Great." Arden shuddered, remembering her first taste of beer under Margo's tutelage. "According to my father, liquor is the first step on the road to hell."

"Not to worry," Luke said as he put his arm around her shoulders. "If this were hell, it would be a lot warmer than this. Besides, you were the one who said you wanted a drink earlier. Why don't you just look at it this way; you'll be drinking to keep warm."

"I'm not too sure about that," Arden said doubtfully. "Anyway, I just realized how hungry I am. I didn't have any dinner. Maybe there's something left over at the gift shop. Their lights are still on, and I can see some people shopping.''

''Okay, but I can sure use a drink,'' Luke answered with a wishful look as they passed the portable bar.

''Oh, look!'' She pointed to a whimsical music box that was playing ''Rudolph the Red Nosed Reindeer.'' A miniature Santa, his sled and the full team of reindeer revolved on the red enamel cover. Humming along with the music, she searched the counters for something edible.

The candy counter was bare except for a few packages of gum. The usual cellophane packets of nuts and pretzels were gone, too. Throughout the shop, there were a few wrapped Christmas presents, the usual I Love New York T-shirts and caps and souvenir trinkets. Newspaper, book and magazine racks were almost bare.

''Don't you have any munchies left?'' Arden asked the weary attendant. ''I'm starved.''

''You and about a thousand other people,'' the clerk answered sympathetically. ''Wait a minute,'' she added as she took in Arden's bedraggled appearance and drooping smile. She disappeared under the counter and came up with a small box of cookies. ''They're stale, but I'm afraid this is it. I was about to throw them away.''

Gingersnaps. The last cookie Arden cared to eat unless she was starving. But these were extenuating circumstances and she *was* starving. She hesitated.

Luke's hand reached over her shoulder and handed the clerk a couple of dollar bills. ''We'll take them,'' he told her. "I'm sure they'll go great with beer. Come on, I don't want to miss out."

He grabbed Arden by the arm and pulled her along after him. The briefcase swung between them, banging against her already sore back, middle and hip. If she weren't black-and-blue on both sides of her body already, Arden was sure she was well on the way.

"Are you sure you can't do something about that briefcase?" she asked.

"Not now," he answered. "We have more important things to worry about."

"You wouldn't think so if you were as bruised as I am," Arden said rubbing her hip.

"Two beers, please," Luke said, ignoring her comment as he elbowed his way to the bar.

"Lucky you came along just now," the bartender announced. "I only have a couple of beers left. To be honest with you," he added, "they're kind of warm. We ran out of ice hours ago."

"I'll take 'em," Luke replied. "They can't be that warm. Not while it's been so cold in here." He reached for his wallet. "Any pretzels?"

"You're kidding!" the jovial man laughed. "I could make a fortune if I had anything fit to eat." He handed Luke change for his twenty and untied his short bartender's apron. "Make yourselves comfortable," he said, gesturing to a small plastic table and chairs alongside the bar. "Guess I can go on home now. That is, if I can make it to the subway. I'll bet half of the city must be holed up down there trying to keep warm."

Arden envied the man. The thought of going home

to a warm house and a festive Christmas Eve dinner was almost too much for her to bear thinking about, especially on an empty stomach. She eyed the open bottle of beer Luke handed her warily.

"What's the matter. Don't you like beer?"

"No," Arden replied. "And I'm afraid it's the only kind of liquor I've tasted before."

"Not even wine?"

"No," she said as she thought of her father's lectures on the subject of alcohol. "My father didn't believe in spirits. Not even coffee, for that matter. Of course, just like anyone else, I've been tempted," she said, remembering her experiment with beer. "In fact, ginger ale with a twist and pink lemonade punch were going to be served at my wedding reception."

"On second thought, maybe you shouldn't start drinking tonight, either," Luke said reaching for the bottle.

"No, really. I want to try it again." She took a deep breath. "As a matter of fact, I intend to start doing a lot of new things after tonight."

No wonder Arden was set on finding excitement, Luke thought as he studied her flushed face. With an upbringing like hers, she was bound to break loose sooner or later. Luckily it was tonight, when he was there to keep an eye out for her.

"Drinking on an empty stomach is the last thing anyone ought to do," he remarked. "Sure you don't want to have a cookie with that?"

Arden gazed down at the warm bottle of beer. Liquor hadn't been on her "wanted" list. Her intentions had been better than that.

Except that her father had always told her the road to hell was paved with good intentions.

Arden raised the tepid bottle to her lips and took an exploratory swallow. She'd had her fill of wise sayings. Enough was enough.

"Ugh!"

Luke offered her a cookie. "Here, eat this. It'll improve the taste."

She bit into the stale gingersnap, wiped crumbs off her chin and shuddered again. "I'm beginning to think maybe my father was right about drinking."

"Maybe so," Luke answered. "But for all the wrong reasons. Here," he added hurriedly when she made another face, "let me take that before you make yourself sick. I can see you're definitely not a beer person."

"How about the champagne?" Arden questioned wistfully.

"Champagne?" Luke glanced at the unopened bottle Arden was still carrying with her. "You heard the guard. The only liquor you can consume on public property is at a bar."

"Then it's okay. This is a bar!"

"I don't think it's a good idea," Luke answered. With all the other things he had to worry about, the last thing he needed was an inebriated Arden.

"Isn't champagne usually served at wedding receptions?"

"Right," Luke agreed reluctantly.

"And weren't we supposed to have been married this afternoon?"

"Sort of, if you want to look at it that way. Here,

have some more cookies while I get the bottle opened." Luke was resigned to his fate. Arden's logic was more right than wrong. "After all, what's a proper wedding celebration without champagne?" he muttered. He went behind the bar and came back with a bottle opener and two plastic glasses.

"You're sure you want to do this?" he asked as he removed the cork, and champagne spurted from the bottle. "Drinking on an empty stomach isn't the brightest idea."

Arden waved her hand airily. "I'll just have one small glass to celebrate the occasion. That can't be enough to make me sick."

"I hope not," Luke prayed under his breath. But it would be just his luck.

"Here." He handed her a glass with an inch of champagne it in. "Go slowly. And if anyone asks you where you got the champagne, I'm going to deny everything."

"I'll drink the evidence," she giggled as the champagne bubbles tickled her nose. "Say, that feels good. How about some more?"

"Sorry," Luke said. "Time to quit while you're ahead of the game."

"Listen," Arden said softly. "It's really Christmas!"

The Honeymoon Express passengers had drifted to an area across from the bar where Arden and Luke were sitting. Accompanied by the guitarist and a CD player, the honeymoon couples had gathered in circles and had formed a choir. Christmas carols filled the air.

"Yes, it is," Luke answered as he glanced at his

wristwatch, grateful, for the moment anyway, there was peace on earth.

If the freak storm hadn't hit the east coast, the tour group would have been gathered under a fake Christmas tree in a tropical setting provided by the tour company. What was a Christmas without snow?

Half an hour later, to the sound of "Silent Night," everyone settled down to sleep on benches and on the floor against the wall. The vacuum cleaner hummed in the background.

Champagne bottle in hand, Luke led Arden to a vacant spot in the corner.

"You know, I have to admit this is the strangest Christmas I've ever spent," Luke remarked when they were settled and he wrapped his overcoat around them. "How about you?"

"One of the best!"

"The best?" Luke looked around at the mass of sleeping people and hundreds more milling in the terminal. "How could this holiday possibly be one of the best?"

"Well," she answered with a shy smile, "I met you."

Luke's heart slipped another notch. Rapidly regretting the impulsive invitation that had brought them together, he was afraid Arden was getting the wrong kind of message. If she thought this arrangement was going to be permanent, she was all wrong.

"Yeah, we met." Luke glanced down at the mop of golden curls nestled under his chin. Her left hand rested on his knee; the bubble-gum-machine wedding ring shone on her finger. She looked like a wife, she acted like a wife.

And he was beginning to feel like a husband.

In spite of all the strange things that had happened to him throughout his years of travel, tonight was fast becoming the most unusual experience of his life.

"You're right," he agreed. "Tonight has been quite an experience, for both of us. Even if we both lost everything we had in the process." *Except for the damn briefcase.*

"Not really," Arden replied with a sleepy sigh. "Those were only material things. Things that money can replace. I don't miss them one bit. What's more important is that I've found I could make it on my own in spite of my father's predictions."

On her own? Taken aback by her comment, Luke looked down at Arden. She may have discovered an inner strength that would carry her through tonight's adventures, but what did she think he'd been doing for her all along?

Chapter Six

She could make it on her own?

Luke smiled to himself, settled back against the wall and looked down at Arden's unruly mop of golden hair resting against his chest. Hair that reminded him of a summer sunset in a tropical sky just before it sank below the horizon in a blaze of color.

He wasn't normally a big believer in fate. Maybe it was the season's air of goodwill that was making him emotional tonight. A feeling he'd taken great care to avoid in his line of business. He'd learned early on never to get too close to anyone. But it was creeping up on him tonight in spite of his good intentions.

Maybe it was because of the way she'd declared her independence to her father on the telephone, or the way she'd jumped to his defense when he was in danger of being arrested that caused him to think of her differently. What was obvious was she was stronger than he'd thought when he'd first laid eyes on her. Considering her background, it took a lot of courage to walk out of her wedding and to confront the law.

Whatever fate had brought them out of a storm and put them here together on Christmas Eve, he was be-

ginning to realize there was more to the woeful bride
than met the eye. If nothing else, she was definitely a
lot more intriguing now than she'd been at first glance.
And that was saying a lot!

A new and unwelcome emotion stirred in his chest
as he realized he'd begun to think about Arden Crandall in a new and disturbing manner.

But as for Arden being able to take care of herself
in the world outside of the airport terminal, that was
a whole different story. He knew from long experience
there were predators out there waiting to eat her innocence alive.

He had only to remember the way she'd taken him
at his word that he was an honest man to know she
was too trusting to be left on her own for the rest of
the night. He was honest, he told himself. At least he
had been until now. But who knew what kind of con
artist might find her later?

Which brought him to the thought that had begun
to trouble him: maybe their paths had crossed for a
reason. Maybe some unknown fate meant him to
watch over her.

It was pretty clear to him, if not to Arden, that she
needed someone to be her tour guide to the real world.
It was also beginning to look as if he was going to
have to be that guide. For now, at least.

He gently brushed his fingers across the soft skin
on her cheek. As much to reassure her as to satisfy a
growing desire to at least touch her skin to see if it
was as soft and silky as he thought it was. Her long
lashes fluttered as she settled back into her dreams.

Not that she wasn't entitled to her dreams. Heck, he

had his own dreams, too. And just as she was set on pursuing hers, he intended to take care of his own—as soon as he delivered her to Cancún.

A man couldn't live on dreams, but, after all, if you didn't have a dream, as the song said, how were you going to make a dream come true? After listening to Arden, maybe it was the same for women.

Thinking about the two of them as a team was probably a losing proposition, anyway, he thought as she stirred against him and murmured in her sleep. Falling for her would be falling for trouble. Especially since she still had her dreams ahead of her. Dreams that would take her down paths he'd already trodden and that he wasn't particularly interested in revisiting.

He gently shifted Arden's head to a more comfortable position on his shoulder and smiled into her hair, when he heard her sleepy murmur of protest.

"Luke?"

"Go back to sleep. Everything's okay," he whispered in her ear. She nodded and drifted back to sleep.

It was just as well. At least she wouldn't be able to discern his growing confusion. A few hours ago, he'd been dead sure about the new life he intended to make for himself. Now even that assurance had begun to dim. He gazed around helplessly, wondering what he'd done to deserve the predicament he'd gotten himself into.

Arden stirred and awakened.

"Cold?" Luke asked her.

"I guess so." She shivered and wiped sleep from her eyes.

Her expression told him the shiver was more than

from the cold. What had she been dreaming of? he wondered, as a blush came over her cheeks.

"Okay, folks, you can go on back to your own gate now," a familiar voice behind Luke announced. "I've finished cleaning up over there. This one is next."

Luke's temper started to simmer. "You're joking!"

"I never joke about my job," the burly maintenance man answered.

"Then, no thanks. And I'm sure I speak for all of us. We'd rather not move. All we want is to be left alone to wait until the airport reopens."

"Sorry, I'm afraid this gate isn't going to be it," the maintenance man replied. "My schedule says I've got to clean up here now."

Luke fished for his wallet and brought out a sizable bill. "Sure I can't persuade you to change your mind?"

"Nope," the man said firmly. "Like I told you, I follow the same routine every night." He glanced at his wristwatch. "Sorry, folks. It's getting late. I've got to get moving."

"What's the point in trying to clean up on a night like this? The area will be a mess in about three minutes flat after we all come back."

"Beats me." The man grinned. "But a job is a job."

Resigned to the inevitable, Luke rose and helped Arden to her feet. "Come on, it looks as if we'll have to find someplace else to keep warm."

Now that Arden was awake, the thought of Luke keeping her warm again sent Arden's blood racing. Just as it had in her dream a few minutes ago, and again when he'd caressed her not realizing she was awake.

Being held in his arms had been okay when she'd been too sleepy to react to his muscular body, his arms holding her, his breath against her hair and the touch of his hands when he'd gently tucked his overcoat closer around them. Her senses had been blurred before, but now she was wide-awake.

"Mr. McCauley," Agnes Chambers, the tour leader, called as she hurried over to join them. "Do you and your wife have a minute?"

The too-familiar question stirred Luke's antennae. What in the blazes had they done now? "I don't know how it's possible to attract so much attention in one night," he muttered, more to himself than Arden. He looked back at the agitated tour leader, who was slowly making her way through sleeping couples to join them.

"What's wrong now, Ms. Chambers?"

"It's just that I remembered you were listed as a single passenger on the manifest," she said eyeing Arden curiously. "Your wife makes an extra person to account for. May I ask your given name, Mrs. McCauley?"

"Arden Crandall...er, McCauley."

The tour guide made a rapid notation.

"Surely that's no problem," Luke interjected. "There must be one extra seat on the plane."

"Actually, there are two, now that I've lost the Travers party!"

"Lost the Travers party?" Arden asked nervously.

"Yes. They were listed as passengers. I've been looking for them for hours."

Arden swallowed the lump that rose in her throat. Travel documents in her purse declared her to be one half of the Travers party. She glanced at a noncommittal Luke. If he thought he'd had enough of trouble, she wasn't going to be the one to remind him there would be even more waiting for him when the plane was ready to depart and the tour leader would check them in.

"Maybe they changed their mind and went back home when they found we weren't going to be able to leave?" Arden said hopefully.

"I'm not sure about that," Agnes Chambers answered. "Not in this kind of weather. Well, maybe they'll turn up before we leave. See you later."

Luke kept his silence. Arden was doing well enough without him. Until he took a good look at her and realized he'd forgotten something.

"Wait here a minute," he told her. "I've some shopping to do." Without a backward glance, he headed for the gift shop where they'd gotten the cookies.

"I need to find something to keep my wife warm," he told the clerk. Wife? Where had that come from?

She gestured to the shop's depleted stock. There were a few I Love NY sweatshirts, caps with the same logo and a number of children's and infants' garments left hanging on the display racks.

He held up a sweatshirt and tried to visualize how Arden might look in it. Even to his inexperienced eye, it looked as if it was miles too large for Arden's small frame and would cover her from neck to toe. A pity, he thought, considering how interesting she looked in her clinging velvet dress. Still, at the rate things were going, he wasn't sure he dared to have her in his arms for the rest of the night without getting into trouble.

"Don't you have something suitable for an adult woman?" he asked. "Something a little warmer and more stylish than this?"

"We did," the clerk answered. "But as soon as the runways shutdown, I sold out of sweaters and scarfs. I guess most everyone realized it was going to be a long, cold night."

"I suppose the sweatshirt will have to do," he finally decided. "Although it looks kind of big."

"It *is* big," she answered cheerfully. "But why don't you look at it this way, it certainly will keep your wife warm."

"How much?" Luke replied, digging into his wallet. This was actually only one of the items he intended to buy for Arden, but first things first. If his shopping spree went on much longer, he'd have to find an ATM or start writing checks. Of course, he realized, either one would leave a trail of his whereabouts behind him. But he couldn't leave Arden shivering, could he?

"Twenty-two dollars. No tax," the clerk grinned. "After all, it's—"

"Yeah, I know," he agreed. "It's Christmas." A Christmas he was going to remember for the rest of his life. "Thanks!"

"Here, put this on," he told Arden when he reached her. "You shouldn't be walking around without something to keep you warm on a night like this. I'd give

you my overcoat if I could take it off," he added helplessly. Frustrated, he gestured with his handcuffed left
hand. The chain rattled, the briefcase bounced in the
air.

Arden winced at the sound. The handcuff, the chain
and the briefcase were definite reminders of Luke's
dark edge. The security guards who seemed to be behind every column in the terminal were another. Did
she really know what she was getting into?

She studied the fleece-lined sweatshirt. If she had a
choice between the shirt and Luke's warmth, she
would have chosen his arms. But she couldn't turn
down his well-meaning gift. Not at the rate the temperature in the terminal seemed to be dropping as the
night went on.

"I should have thought of it myself," she muttered,
putting the thought of his arms out of her mind. How
quickly she'd forgotten she should put the brakes on
her growing response to Luke's strong male appeal.
"How much do I owe you?"

"No, really, it's on me," he said, as she thrust a
twenty-dollar bill toward him. "Actually, I owe you."

"For what?"

"You saved me from the law," he replied with a
wry grin. "With the way my luck was going, I'd probably be spending Christmas in the slammer if you
hadn't spoken up for me."

"The slammer?" Her brow wrinkled. "I'm afraid I
don't understand."

"Jail, to you," he said, thinking of how sheltered
she must have been and what a different world awaited

her. "Stepping in and telling the law you're my wife took a lot of courage."

"I only did what I felt I had to do," she answered. "What's right is right. I couldn't let him arrest you just because you resembled some criminal, and without any real proof, could I?"

"Is that the only reason you spoke up?" Luke asked. What devil was driving him to play a game with her?

"Not at all," she answered. A faint blush told him she knew this was a game. "After he said I fit the description of the wanted man's female accomplice, I expected to be arrested myself."

His sable eyes bored into hers. How could he tell her how reluctant he was to face the rest of the night without her in his arms? He had to let her go. Now was as good a time as any.

"Still, it was a brave thing to do," he assured her. "For all you knew, I *could* have been the guy in the Wanted poster."

Arden shuddered at the reminder.

She, too, could have ended up in jail, or at least down at the police station for questioning.

And Luke? She recalled the doubt in the security officer's eyes when he questioned them. And the way the man still dogged their footsteps. If she didn't want to be the one to put Luke in jeopardy, she'd have to stay.

Arden could see by the expression on Luke's face that his thoughts paralleled her own.

"Actually, I've been thinking," she said. "Perhaps

we should stick together tonight, after all. I'm willing to be Mrs. McCauley until we get to Cancún.''

''I'm glad to hear that,'' he said gravely. ''I've been told there's safety in numbers. Mr. and Mrs. McCauley it is.''

''Wait a minute,'' Arden said sternly. Caution was better late than never. ''Let me finish. I intend this to be a purely business relationship from now on.''

''Right,'' he replied, relieved that the sexual tension that had grown between them was over. ''You have my word on it. Here, put the sweatshirt on over your dress before you catch cold. Then we'll find a place where we can hole up for the rest of the night.''

''In plain sight?''

''Of course,'' he answered. ''In plain sight.''

He wasn't sure what was bothering her, but if hanging around in plain sight was what she wanted, that's what she was going to have. Personally he would have preferred being somewhere out of sight where the security staff couldn't find them.

Arden was relieved. There *was* safety in numbers, although not for the reason Luke may have thought. Now that they'd declared some kind of truce and would spend the rest of the night together in the open, she felt protected from the irresistible attraction she felt for Luke. And hopefully safe from the security guards who kept popping up to question them.

Independence was fine, but not if it landed her in jail.

The sweatshirt, when she put it on, hung over her hands and down to her knees. Her velvet wedding dress had shrunk and hung in uneven lengths around her ankles. Chagrined at her appearance, she pictured the way she must look to Luke. Until she saw the interest grow in his eyes.

Mental danger signals sounded. If Luke was as interested in her as she was in him, she was headed for trouble.

"Come on," he urged. "Let's find a place where I don't stick out like a sore thumb. I'm beat."

So was she, Arden sighed as she gazed around the terminal. Fellow travelers had settled down for the night. Voices were subdued, the sounds of Christmas were fading.

She followed Luke to the corner where they'd first met and where the night had started. Deep in thought, she slowed.

Luke noticed she wasn't at his side. He swung around. Arden lagged behind him. Worry lines creased her forehead.

"Something wrong?" he asked as he turned back to join her.

"No, not really."

Not really? If ever he'd seen a woman with something on her mind, it was Arden.

"Come on now," he teased. "I wasn't born yesterday. I know a problem when I see it. You're not still worried about your father's health, are you?"

"No, I'm sure he'll be fine as soon as he gets over last night's excitement."

Luke studied her for a long moment. "So what's the matter? You look kind of funny. Aren't you feeling well?"

She felt kind of funny, too. Torn between trying to

hide her mixed feelings about him and the urge to tell him the truth about her thoughts, she decided to choose the middle ground. After all, outside of his being chained to a briefcase, Luke hadn't said or done anything to alarm her. So far he'd been decent. And even though she was sure she could have seen the night through by herself, he was a welcome companion.

It was the future she was starting to worry about.

What would be the use of falling for a man who'd made it clear he was going his own way after tomorrow?

She said the first thing that popped into her mind. "I was just thinking what a wonderful night this is."

"A wonderful night this is?" Luke glanced at his wristwatch. "Outside of being holed up here for at least eight hours without something decent to eat or drink, or even a place to relax, what's so wonderful about tonight?"

"It's the reminder that it's Christmas morning, or will be in a few hours," she answered. She gestured to where one whimsical passenger had built a small snowman with real snow he'd brought from outside the terminal. "Only, Christmas is a time to be with your family," she added wistfully.

"I thought that you and I were a family," Luke joked.

He could tell from the wary look that came into her eyes he may have said the wrong thing.

"What would people think if they knew the truth about us?"

"What truth?"

"That we're really not married."

Luke eyed her thoughtfully. Her shimmering blue eyes drew him deeper than he wanted himself to be drawn. Innocent intentions or not, he had the alarming premonition that if anyone could mess up his plans, it would be Arden.

"Since you've spent most of the night in my arms, I'm sure no one will think anything of it," he answered lightly. "After all, we *are* supposed to be married."

Arden felt herself blush. The word *marriage* started a whole new train of thought that excited even as it worried her. Thoughts she couldn't afford to picture, let alone think about. Not with Luke as her husband. Not when the twinkle in his eyes was more suggestion than laughter.

A spark of excitement ignited in her middle. She knew she'd have to put out the fire unless she was ready to let her heart lead her deeper into this relationship. Make-believe or not. And with a man she only half trusted.

She'd never felt this way before, she realized. John had been very proper and had treated her as if she were a vestal virgin. Virgin she might be, but she'd always felt there was more to life than living on the pedestal where he'd put her.

With Luke, somehow it was different. He made her feel alive.

"I wasn't thinking along those lines," she said, avoiding his gaze in case her intimate thoughts were written in her eyes. "I was thinking about my family, and the way we gathered around the tree on Christmas morning to open our gifts before we went to church.''

"Arden," Luke explained patiently, "in case you haven't noticed, there is no Christmas tree, no gifts, and although there may be a chapel around, we are in an airport waiting for clearance to leave the country. We are not going to go to church, either. We're going to Cancún.''

In spite of the smile Arden had pasted on her lips, Luke sensed something *was* wrong. For one thing, the smile was obviously a phony. And then there was the way she kept twisting the ersatz wedding ring around her finger. For another, she clutched her purse to her chest in a way that told him she was a hundred-and-twenty-pound bundle of anxiety waiting to explode. Or maybe a little less, he thought as he remembered the way the wilted velvet wedding dress had drooped limply around her slender figure exposing every delectable curve.

As far as he could tell, Arden Crandall was definitely not okay.

For the first time in a long time, he recalled the love and laughter of his own Christmas mornings as a youngster. The tree with the popcorn and cranberry garlands he and his sister had strung every year. The hot chocolate with tiny marshmallows floating on top his mother prepared for the family to ward off the early-morning cold as they gathered under the gaily decorated tree. And his young sister's delight when their father, masquerading as Santa Claus in a rented suit, passed out gifts.

What the heck, he thought, maybe she was right

about Christmas. Maybe it wasn't only for kids. If it took a Christmas tree and a few small gifts to make her happy, by God, he was going to see to it the smile on her face became real. Considering the traumatic phone call she'd had with her father and the unwitting part he'd played in her problems tonight, he felt he owed her that much.

The food concessions were still closed, Luke noted regretfully as they walked through the terminal, so hot chocolate was out. He wasn't going to pretend he was Santa Claus, either, but he was pretty sure he could take care of the rest of the setting.

"Come on, let's go," he said as he started off.

"Go?" Arden hung back. "Go where?"

"Shopping," he called over his shoulder.

Arden had to pick up her skirts and run to keep up with him. "Again?"

"You'll see."

The gift shop was still open. He'd been right, Luke thought gratefully as his eyes searched the counters. No merchant in his right mind was going to close on a night like tonight. Not when there were hundreds of captive shoppers, and definitely not until the shelves were bare.

"Wait out here a minute," he told Arden. He intended to make sure this holiday wasn't going to be different for her than other Christmas mornings. Christmas gifts were supposed to be a surprise.

He noted the way she hesitated, as if uncertain as to whether or not to wait. "I won't be long," he called out to her. She rewarded him with an uncertain smile.

Thankfully, the gift he'd had in mind was still there.

Luke made straight for the counter and picked up the Santa Claus music box he'd seen earlier. He turned it over, wound the key. The tiny sled started to move across miniature tracks on the top of the box to the music of "Rudolph the Red Nosed Reindeer." With a satisfied smile, Luke handed it to the smiling clerk who'd waited on him earlier.

"You again?" she commented.

"Yeah. I thought I'd buy my wife a few gifts to make up for having to wait until morning to leave on our honeymoon."

"No problem," the clerk answered. "We have to help each other out at times like this." She smiled sympathetically and waved to Arden who was waiting outside the shop. "It's no way to start a honeymoon, is it? I'm sure glad my own started out better than this."

"It's going to be a night to remember, all right." Luke agreed. If she only knew the whole of it! The briefcase chained to his wrist, the suspicious glances and questions had been enough to try any man. Especially when he wasn't guilty of any wrongdoing— yet. Of course, there *was* Arden to make up for some of it. Even if she was only a temporary diversion.

"Yeah. Think of all the great stories you can tell your children someday," the clerk responded cheerfully. "They'll never believe it!"

Children? Luke shuddered. He was in this caper only as long as it would take to get Arden to Cancún and say goodbye before he took off for parts unknown. He kept that detail to himself.

"Wait a minute." He found himself reaching to a

display shelf to take down a fake miniature Christmas tree. It was adorned with red and white garlands that reminded him of the Christmas trees of his own childhood. "I'll take this, too, if it's for sale."

"It is now," the clerk assured him. "The sooner I sell out, the sooner I can go home to my own husband. We've only been married for a few months, and I sure didn't want to work tonight. Christmas Eve is no night to spend by yourself, is it?"

"No, it's not," Luke replied. He could write a book on the many empty Christmas Eves he'd spent alone. Somehow, this one promised to be a little happier.

He glanced over his shoulder at Arden who was watching him curiously. She *had* made this holiday memorable, at that.

He inventoried his purchases.

The small tree was for the true spirit of Christmas.

The music box was for the child in Arden.

There was one thing still lacking.

Perfume for the woman within her!

White Diamonds or Passion in their fashionable packaging looked appropriate for a bride. He glanced back again to where Arden waited. *Passion?* Not for the Arden he knew. Maybe she could be capable of passion with the right man, but it wasn't going to be him. Not that a part of him he was trying to ignore didn't wish he could be the one to share a night of passion with her.

Under the circumstances, maybe he shouldn't open the subject by giving Arden perfume with such a sensuous name tag.

Luke thoughtfully surveyed the boxes of perfume

displayed in the counter in front of him. Even if she'd probably wonder why a new groom didn't know his bride well enough to make a suitable choice, he had to ask the clerk which scent was appropriate for a new bride.

"Oh, White Diamonds, by all means," the clerk replied when he asked the question. She reached for a sample of the perfume and sprayed it on the back of his hand. "Diamonds are forever," she went on, "long after the first passion of marriage passes." She held up her own diamond wedding ring for him to see.

Forever? echoed in Luke's thoughts as he sniffed the perfume. Its fragrance was just strong enough to sharpen his senses and to suggest nights of desire. But *forever* was a long time, longer than he intended. Certainly more than the few hours still ahead of him before the flight to Cancún and a quick goodbye to his "bride."

On the other hand, White Diamonds had a nice ring to it. Especially since he hadn't given his temporary "bride" a wedding ring remotely resembling anything of value.

"I'll take it," he said, indicating a small bottle of the perfume. "How much do I owe you?"

She named a sum. Considering the smile he thought would come over Arden's face when she saw the presents he was buying for her, they would have been cheap at twice the price.

"The store will take care of the sales tax as its wedding present to you and your wife. Just don't tell the boss," the clerk laughed. "If you wait a minute, I'll wrap everything for you and put them in a nice little holiday shopping bag.''

Luke dug into his wallet for the money. It was almost ATM time.

Chapter Seven

"Something's wrong," Arden said under her breath when he came back to her.

Luke froze. What could have happened during the few minutes he was in the gift shop? "What kind of trouble?"

"Them," she whispered. He followed her gaze. Sure enough, two security guards were standing a short distance away trying to be inconspicuous. What had they thought he was going to do, rob the shop with hundreds of people around?

"Forget them," he assured her. "You don't have anything to worry about and neither do I."

"You're sure?"

"I'm sure. Here, these are for you."

He handed her the small, decorated shopping bag with a flourish. "Merry Christmas," he said. When her eyes lit up, he gave in to the spirit of the holiday and kissed her lightly on the cheek.

This time the smile that came across Arden's face was real. And so was the way a single dimple danced across her cheek at his brief kiss. She was so easy to please that it warmed Luke's cynical heart.

"Feeling better?" he asked, fighting the desire to gather her in his arms for a Christmas kiss they would both remember. She might be smiling, but something was still missing in her smile.

"Yes, thank you," she replied. "Now, it's beginning to feel like Christmas!"

"Good," he answered thankfully. "So now do you want to tell me what's on your mind?"

"I've already told you," Arden said, fingering the brightly wrapped packages and avoiding his eyes.

"No, that was just an excuse not to tell me," he chided. "Come on now. New wives shouldn't keep secrets from their grooms," Luke added playfully. "It's a heck of a way to start married life, especially on the first night of the honeymoon."

"It's not really my honeymoon," she corrected in a small, tight voice.

He hadn't really thought for a minute she'd been thinking of her aborted honeymoon. So what had he said to set her off again?

Good Lord, he thought with a growing awareness of how she might have taken his remark. She didn't believe he was going to press her for an actual honeymoon, did she?

"Look, I know we're only pretending to be newlyweds," Luke assured her. He led her to a more secluded corner. "Why don't you open your gifts now? Or, if you like, you can wait until morning.

He found an empty bench. "Now it doesn't take a mind reader to know something is on your mind. I'm sure it'll make both of us happier if you let me in on the secret."

Arden met his probing gaze. How could she tell him he was only part of the problem that troubled her? And that her own awakened senses were the rest?

"I really don't know if I can explain it to you," she answered.

"Try me."

"I'm afraid I can't," she said, twisting the ribbon on the gift bag. "Not when I can hardly understand it myself."

Luke carefully studied the uneasiness in her eyes as he wondered what on earth could be still bothering her.

Her reputation?

Hardly likely, considering the way she'd stood up to her aunt Jane and her father's thundering accusations.

Her father?

No, she'd sounded pretty resolute when she'd told him she intended to be her own woman. Of course she cared about her father, but how much did the man care for his daughter to put her through the wringer like he did? Did he realize how deeply he had hurt her?

Was it the thought of Christmas morning and the gifts that would have been waiting for her under the tree at home until she returned from her honeymoon with John Travers?

No, he didn't think so. Not after he'd seen the passing look of delight on her face and in her eyes when he'd handed her her gifts. And certainly not in the way she'd described her fiancé. But her expression still remained troubled.

"Still having second thoughts about running out on your wedding?"

"No." Arden shook her head. "Definitely not!"

By now, he'd mentioned everything he could think of that could be bothering her. Except for one.

That left him as her problem.

A quick mental review of their recent conversation gave him a possible, though astounding, answer. Was it something about him that bothered her?

"Arden, look at me," he commanded. "Are you afraid of me? Of being alone with me?"

Honest to the core, Arden met his eyes and found herself telling him the truth. Or at least part of it. "Truthfully, maybe I was for a few minutes back there, but I'm not anymore."

"Thank goodness for that," he remarked ruefully. "I'd hate to think I was the type who scared people."

"Maybe it's just that I don't really know you very well," she answered as she glanced at the briefcase he clutched in his left hand. The handcuff was hidden by his sleeve, but it was there.

"You have nothing to worry about, I swear," Luke replied as he followed her gaze. His good humor began to fade. Hadn't he shown her he was no threat, to her or to anyone else? He may be damned by the briefcase, but he'd expected her to trust him by now.

"So, there *is* something bothering you," he said as he eyed her thoughtfully. A crazy idea shot out of the blue like a thunderbolt and hit him right between the eyes. An impossible idea but just bizarre enough to be true. At the thought, an unexpected wave of desire washed over him.

"Is it this?" he asked as he put a forefinger under her chin and tipped her face to his for a kiss.

Her lips opened in a soundless answer. Without a second thought, Luke gave in to temptation.

He brushed her ruby red lips with his own. In seconds he knew one kiss wasn't going to be enough.

"Or this?"

This time he let his kiss grow bolder. His tongue probed the sides of her lips, wandered until her lips opened to give him entry.

With a groan, he took her face between his two hands and kissed her deeply. The kiss was a mixture of his frustration and desire. Frustration because he couldn't afford to have the kiss mean anything, and a desire he couldn't ignore. The sensuous fragrance of the White Diamonds perfume the shop clerk had sprayed on the back of his hand heightened his desire for her.

Her tentative response was all he needed to kiss her again.

Arden forced herself to face the truth. It wasn't Luke she was afraid of, it was his attraction for her that worried her. And her response to the myriad new emotions coursing over her when he kissed her. She'd dreamed of such an embrace in her fanciful daydreams, but now it was coming true in a way she'd never expected.

She stepped closer into his embrace, thirsty for the friction of his lips on hers, the strangely erotic taste of gingersnaps and warm beer on his breath, the scent of perfume on his hands. She'd never felt like this before, never been kissed like this before. And, in truth, had never expected to be. Certainly not by John, a dear but unimaginative man.

She closed her eyes, the better to let herself be plunged into the sea of sensation that swept her from head to toe and lingered in her middle.

She would never be able to think of Luke in an impersonal way again.

When the kiss was over, Luke gently stroked the sides of her brow with his thumbs and lightly kissed the path his fingers had taken. He folded her into his arms until his heart could stop racing and his pragmatic mind took over. "What are you doing to me?" he asked, even as he held her closer to him.

He hadn't intended his embrace to be so sure, so strong. He hadn't even meant his kisses to be more than teasing questions. And all because he'd been frustrated and angry at the thought Arden was afraid of him. But her lips had looked so soft, so warm, so inviting, he couldn't help himself. Now, looking down into her glowing eyes, he realized he may have gone farther than he'd intended.

With a sinking feeling, he drew away. He shouldn't have kissed her so passionately, or touched her to begin with. Not when her response to his embrace was so telling. And not when he couldn't afford to have her believe his kisses and the embrace meant anything serious.

"I suppose that shouldn't have happened," he said ruefully. "But actually, I have to be honest with you and admit that I'm not sorry it did."

"I'm not sorry, either," she answered, rubbing her

fingers across her bruised lips. "I guess we both got carried away by the Christmas spirit in the air."

It was true. She wasn't sorry. Not a bit. His had been her first real passionate kisses, and now that she'd tasted of their pleasure, she was looking forward to more. If it wasn't meant to be with Luke as her lover, then as soon as she found the right man to share those kisses with.

Except that it was too late. She'd already lost her heart in the depths of Luke's sable eyes.

Luke cleared his throat. "Come on, let's go back and see if we can find someplace to spend the rest of the night."

It didn't take long for Luke to realize there was no such place.

"Maybe we ought to try to get back home tonight instead of waiting for the flight to leave," a male voice on the other side of Luke suggested. He turned around, but the comment hadn't been directed to him. The man had spoken to his very pregnant wife.

"But this is our honeymoon!" the bride in the man's arms declared. "I've been looking forward to it for a long time!"

"I know, sweetheart, but in your condition maybe it's not such a good idea to hang around here any longer. All this excitement might be bad for the baby."

"Don't be silly, Larry. The baby isn't due for two weeks. We're only going to be away for five days."

Luke snapped to attention. His mental alarm bells went off. Her baby was due in two weeks?

He cautiously eyed the bride. It was the first time

he'd ever seen an expectant mother wearing a maternity wedding dress. Her husband was right. Sitting on a cold floor waiting for their flight to leave couldn't have been a good idea for the mother, or the unborn child. Just as taking off for a foreign country at thirty thousand feet in the air was another fool idea. He was willing to bet the charter airline personnel hadn't been aware of just how pregnant this particular bride was.

He exchanged sympathetic glances with the harried groom.

All things considered, he thought, with another apprehensive glance at the pregnant bride, he would rather be sitting somewhere else.

"What's going on over there?" Arden whispered in his ear.

"Nothing, I hope," he answered with a quick glance at Arden's flat middle. Thank goodness *she* wasn't pregnant. From what he knew about her, if ever a woman had walked the straight and narrow path until now, Arden had to be one of them. But if she kept draping herself over a man like she was doing to him, she was going to be in for a big surprise one of these days. Hadn't she ever heard about the birds and the bees?

"Ouch! That hurt!"

From the surprise in the pregnant bride's tone of voice, and the way she grabbed her middle, Luke had the sinking feeling the moment of reckoning was near, if it hadn't already arrived.

In a flash of déjà vu, his past experience surfaced.

It had been in a small city in the Central American country of Guatemala. Working for the federal government, he'd been hot on the trail of a suspected drug smuggler. The guy, who obviously knew where he was going, had disappeared into the jungle. Tired, worn and new to the area, Luke had rented a Jeep and set out to track him.

What he *had* found was a broken-down cart alongside an overgrown road with an elderly woman, two small children and their pregnant mother. Realizing he wasn't going to find his man, Luke had used the Spanish he knew to offer to give them a lift to the nearest town and, hopefully, a hospital. With the mother protesting the baby wasn't due yet, and the kids hollering their heads off, they hadn't gotten very far.

With the help of the weathered old woman, the baby had been born in the back of the Jeep.

But this wasn't a Central American jungle, and there wasn't anyone to give him instructions.

One experience like that was enough for him to swear off marriage and fatherhood and never to put a woman through the trauma of childbirth. He'd also learned babies usually had their own agenda.

The way his luck had been going lately, the kid was bound to arrive tonight.

"Jenny?" The prospective father questioned apprehensively as he started to rub his wife's hands. "Are you all right?"

Based on what he remembered seeing on TV, Luke knew the guy should have been rubbing his bride's back, if he was going to rub her anywhere. Better still, he should have been calling 911. Or at least Airport Security. But from the way things were beginning to look, it was probably already too late.

Resigned to the inevitable, Luke bestirred himself.

"How long have you been having pains, Mrs...."

"Alcott, and the pains have been strong for the last three hours," the woman gasped and winced again. "Why, are you a doctor?"

"No," Luke replied. He uttered a silent prayer. "But unless I miss my guess, I'm about as good a one as you're likely to get under the circumstances until your husband can find a real one. With the airport crowded this way, any medics around probably have their hands full."

"I'm her husband. Do we have time to take my wife to a hospital?" her groom asked, casting a worried look at his laboring wife. "She looks awful."

"Awful! Why, Larry Alcott, what a terrible thing to say! It's your baby I'm having!" his wife shouted in between groans.

"I didn't mean it the way it sounds, sweetheart. It's just that things are happening sooner than I thought they would. And I never thought they would happen in a place like this or we wouldn't have come here!"

Luke turned back to Arden and spoke in an undertone. "See if you can get someone to use the PA system for a doctor or a nurse. And while you're at it, find out if there are any medical emergency teams in the terminals tonight. As for you, Alcott, maybe you'd better call 911."

"Oh, my!" Jenny Alcott reached for her husband's hand as another pain gripped her. "That was one of the worst! Don't you dare leave me, Larry!"

Her husband's face turned as white as his wife's

wedding dress. "Why didn't you tell me sooner? We could have gotten to a hospital by now!"

"I just thought it was false labor because of the excitement of our wedding. I didn't want to miss our honeymoon!"

"Gosh, Jenny. I knew we should have gone straight home after the ceremony. Maybe we still can." Her husband looked frantic.

"Mr. Alcott," Luke interjected as he felt a dampness spread against his knee. "I think it's a little late for that." He took one of Jenny Alcott's hands in his and squeezed his reassurance. "Don't worry. Everything is going to be okay, you'll see. At a time like this, it's important to stay calm."

"I know," she answered between groans, "but it hurts!"

"It's supposed to," he answered gently as he remembered the big birth scene in the TV movie he'd watched a few nights ago. "Been to a Lamaze class lately?" he asked her husband.

"Sure."

One look at the guy and Luke didn't know who was worse off, the husband or the wife! Alcott didn't look as if he remembered much of what he'd learned at class, either.

"Then maybe the two of you ought to begin some of those breathing exercises you've been practicing."

With a nervous glance at each other, the bride and her groom set themselves to breathing in unison.

Luke removed the scarf around his neck and loosened his tie ready to go to work. He swore under his breath when the chain attached to his wrist pulled his briefcase into view. He shrugged helplessly. Helping Jenny Alcott give birth wasn't going to be easy with that damn briefcase getting in the way. And the groom's anxious glances at Luke's wrist wasn't helping.

Larry Alcott paused in midbreath. "Who are you, anyway? And what's that around your wrist, a handcuff?" He struggled to his feet. "Maybe I ought to call 911, after all," he said as the chain on Luke's wrist rattled.

"No one who ought to worry you," Luke answered as he struggled to be firm, yet compassionate. "Arden, why don't you come over here and keep Mrs. Alcott busy?" he added wearily, noticing for the first time the small crowd of fellow travelers who had gathered around him and the Alcotts. There was no doubt in his mind he was going to be remembered for life because of that damn briefcase, and now the birth of the Alcott baby. But he didn't have the luxury of being able to feel sorry for himself. He had a more urgent problem on his mind right now.

Arden hastily nodded and went around Luke to hold Jenny Alcott's hand. Not that it seemed to help much, but the woman's husband was too distracted to help. After glancing at his wife and back to Luke's wrist, Alcott looked ready to faint.

"Okay, Mr. Alcott, get in behind your wife and hold her between your legs." He turned to the nearest onlooker. "How about someone calling 911? And maybe some of you can rig up a makeshift curtain with your raincoats and give Mrs. Alcott some privacy?"

Half a dozen travelers scrambled to help. In no time,

Luke, Arden and the Alcotts were behind a screen made of raincoats, overcoats and jackets.

"Breathe! Breathe!" he instructed as he peered under the bride's maternity dress.

"I'm trying to, dammit, but the pain keeps getting in the way," Jenny Alcott answered. "Oh, dear, I'm sorry I said that. But—"

"Don't worry about it, I've heard worse cuss words with a lot less reason," Luke assured her. "But if it will make you feel better, go ahead." He looked at Jenny. "Someone go and see if Airport Security can bring some emergency aid over here right away." A helpful groom took off at a run. "Arden, think you could help me when I tell you to?"

"Of course," she replied. "I used to volunteer at our senior retirement home."

"Well," Luke answered dryly. "I don't imagine there was much of this type of activity going on over there. But in the meantime why don't you take up a collection of clean, white handkerchiefs."

"I can go and get some paper towels out of the rest room," a breathless onlooker offered. "Will that help?"

"It's better than nothing," Luke agreed. He turned back to the Alcotts. "Breathe!"

Larry Alcott looked too frightened to move, let alone breathe.

"I am, I am," Jenny shouted, "but it's not helping. It still hurts!"

"Sorry," Luke offered, thinking rapidly. "Mr. Alcott, please give your wife your leather belt to chew on. On the other hand," he amended as he checked the progress of the birth, "it doesn't look as if this is going to go on much longer."

"She's really going to have the baby right here, isn't she?" Larry Alcott looked as if he was about to pass out. Luke didn't blame him. He'd felt the same way when he'd helped deliver the baby down in Guatemala.

"Looks like it," Luke answered. He took the paper towels and placed them under Jenny. That taken care of, he took the handkerchiefs Arden had collected and made ready to put them under the straining mother when the time arrived.

"Airport Security says they're sorry," the breathless man who'd run for help announced. "The medics are too busy to come over right now. They're short of staff because of the Christmas holiday and there's more medical emergencies going on than they can handle."

"Did you tell them there's a woman here about to have a baby?"

"Yeah. When I described what was going on, they said to tell you that as long as you knew how to handle the birth go ahead and they'd have someone here as soon as they could."

He knew how to handle it? Not any more than he would have known what to do in a tropical jungle without the old lady's help.

Jenny Alcott groaned again and strained against her husband.

"Wait a minute," Luke told the panting mother. "Don't push just yet. Not until I tell you to."

"What do you mean, don't push?" she shouted. "I can't stop!"

"I can see the baby's head," Luke finally announced. "When you feel the next pain, *then* you can push."

He could feel Arden tense at his side. "Ever seen a baby born before?" he asked.

"No. And it's not something anyone I know talks about, either," she whispered.

"Maybe you shouldn't be watching this. Why don't you just concentrate on keeping the briefcase out of the way?"

"I will, but I want to watch," she answered, her voice soft and shaken. "It's a Christmas miracle."

The awe in her voice decided Luke. If Arden was strong enough to witness a child being born, maybe she *was* strong enough to see herself through her dreams for the future. And maybe, for her, this was her first adventure. As for himself, he would have been willing to forgo this one.

"Okay, you can stay, but see if you can keep that damn briefcase out of my way." He turned back to Jenny Alcott.

"There, that's enough," he announced a few minutes later. "The baby is being born right... about...now! It's a boy!" He busied himself wrapping the little guy in the handkerchiefs Arden had rounded up.

A cheer went up from the crowd. Someone shouted, "Merry Christmas!"

The father took one look at the bloodied infant and promptly fainted.

"What are you going to do with my husband?" Jenny Alcott asked, reaching for her new son and gazing down at her groom.

"Forget the poor guy for now." Luke laughed, looking down at the prone man. "He's probably better off out of it. For that matter, you are, too."

Luke turned to Arden. "You can let go of the briefcase for now. How about getting the shoestring off my shoe?"

"Shoestring? What in heaven's name are you going to do with a shoestring at a time like this?"

"Never mind," he answered. "Just do it. I'll explain later."

He wiped off the squalling infant with the donated handkerchiefs, grinning as he dodged flailing tiny arms and legs. Poor little guy, he didn't like the public attention he was getting any more than Luke did.

When Arden handed him the shoestring, Luke tied the baby's umbilical cord in two places. He took his pocket knife out of his pants pocket and cut the cord in between the two knots. He swore under his breath at the damn briefcase hanging from his wrist that was driving him nuts.

"What's going on here?" A security officer pushed his way to the front of the crowd and eyed Luke. "Oh, it's you again?"

"Yeah," Luke replied with a wry shrug of his shoulders. "Although I'd much rather it would have been someone else."

The officer took in the situation at a glance, extracted his cellular phone and called for help. "Someone ought to be here soon. Got everything in hand?"

"Almost. Arden, how about getting me that bottle of champagne over there?"

"Champagne?" the officer questioned. "Isn't it a little too soon to start toasting the little guy?"

"Not yet," Luke assured him. "I have a better use for it."

"You're not going to drink it?" a horrified Arden asked.

"No, but it's not a bad idea," Luke muttered. "Right now the champagne will work as an antiseptic until we can get a real one."

"Wait a minute!" The revived groom stirred, sat up and looked around. "Did I hear you say I have a son?"

"Sure do," Luke said, wiping his hands off with a clean handkerchief. "Looks like a big, healthy one, at that."

"Jenny!" Larry sprang to his feet and rushed to his wife's side. "You okay?"

"Yes, honey," his happy wife answered. "And so is your new son." She held him up for her husband to see.

The new father turned to Luke. "What did you say your name was?"

"Luke McCauley." Luke answered before he realized what the question could mean: newspaper headlines trumpeting a Christmas miracle at JFK! At the rate things were going, he would have enough notoriety to put him on the front page of every daily paper.

"I don't know how to thank you," Alcott said effusively, trying to shake Luke's hand. "I'd like to name my son after you."

"Thanks," Luke replied, gathering up his scarf and tie. "But I already have a namesake." Down in Guatemala. He didn't need another. In fact, he was considering changing his name. Everyone in the state of New York would know it over their morning coffee.

"How about calling him Noel?" Arden suggested as she glanced at her wristwatch. "It's past midnight. Today is Christmas."

"I'd like that." Jenny Alcott beamed. "We'll call the baby Noel Lawrence Alcott, if you're sure you don't want us to call him after you, Mr. McCauley. I want to thank you, and your wife, too."

Wife? Luke cast an eye at a shaken but happy Arden. A simple impulse was rapidly turning into a marriage!

The medical crew arrived in time to prevent Arden from answering. Just as well, she thought, eyeing a weary Luke. The last thing he appeared to want was a wife. And the last thing she wanted was a husband, fake or not. She would stay out of his way as long as he stayed out of hers.

"Here we are, better late than never!" a cheery voice announced. Two airport emergency medics arrived with a wheelchair and medical kits. A quick check told them nature had taken its course, with a little bit of help from Luke.

"Looks like one of you did a great job! Who's the hero?"

"He is!" A dozen fingers pointed to Luke.

"Congratulations, it looks as if you've done quite a job for an amateur. We'll have someone along in a few minutes to take a report. In the meantime we'll take the lady and the baby to the hospital for a checkup. Who's the father?''

Larry Alcott identified himself, gathered up their belongings and, with a happy wave, followed the medics.

"How did you know what to do?" Arden asked Luke as they made their way to the rest rooms to clean up.

"Don't ask," he answered. "This is the sort of experience I'd just as soon forget."

"But you *have* done this before, haven't you?"

"Arden," he said just as he entered the men's room. "Leave it alone. The less you know about me, the better."

Chapter Eight

Six feet of blue uniform, gleaming badge and a nasty smile: Airport Security again! This one waited for him at the door to the rest room when he made his exit. Luke shouldn't have been surprised, but he was damn tired of the whole mess.

"Your wife told me I could find you here," the man said with a twist of his mouth when he said wife. "I'll need some information from you for a report."

"Report? What kind of report?" Luke rapidly searched his memory. He'd already filled out all the necessary declarations when he'd turned in the gun he'd pick up at his destination. As for the stolen luggage caper, Arden had taken care of that. What kind of report did the City of New York want from him now?

"We need to make out a report about the kid you helped bring into the world," the guard said with a smirk.

The baby? "Jenny Alcott brought it into the world. All I did was be there for her when there wasn't anyone else around to handle it," Luke answered. He was trying to be patient, but enough was enough. For a bachelor and an amateur in the maternity world at that, helping little Noel into the world was two kids too many.

"Still, it *was* you, wasn't it?"

Luke wasn't sure which unlucky star he'd been born under, but it looked as if it was positioned firmly over his head. At the rate things were going, if the guard chose to follow the rules, he could be arrested for practicing medicine without a license.

"Yes," Luke answered, resigned to the inevitable. "Now, what's this about a wife?"

"The little lady back there." With a frown, the security guard gestured to where Arden was hovering in the background.

"Oh, *that* wife," Luke answered. In all the excitement of delivering Noel he'd forgotten the agreement he'd made with Arden to pass as husband and wife for the duration. In spite of playing at being her groom all night, he hadn't quite gotten around to thinking of himself as her husband.

There was no denying he hadn't been able to cool the growing attraction between them. It presented a complication he had to face, the sooner the better. Not only was the charade cramping his style, pretending to be her husband wasn't fair to Arden. What if she took the whole thing seriously?

A skeptical look crossed the guard's face. "Haven't been married long enough to remember you have a wife?"

Hell! Luke recognized a snide remark when he heard it. Somehow, he'd managed to add more fuel to the man's suspicions. Namely, who Luke was and

what he was doing here. Just his luck! A quick glance
at the frowning guard's left hand told Luke the guy
was married.

"Hardly," Luke joked when what he really wanted
to do was punch the guy out. Not just him—he was
tired and disgusted enough to take on anyone who
crossed him. He gritted his teeth and made a show of
glancing at his watch. "It hasn't even been twenty-
fours hours since I gave up my freedom. Hell, as a
married man, you ought to know what I mean!"

"Yeah, I guess so." The man's reluctant smile was
faint, but Luke knew he'd hit the guy where it hurt.
"I've been married to the same woman for thirty-five
years and it took ten of them to get used to having a
wife," the man said ruefully. "Give yours a little time
and she'll never let you forget her again."

Luke nodded politely.

"Say, about that briefcase you have chained to your
wrist…"

Luke closed his eyes. If he didn't get rid of that
damn briefcase pretty soon, he *was* going to hit the
next guy who had a smart remark to make. Except that
he'd probably land in jail. No matter how he cut it, he
couldn't wait for the night to end so he could be on
his way.

"Didn't anyone tell you they don't use handcuffs
anymore?"

"Sure," Luke replied wearily and took a firmer grip
on the briefcase handle. If the smirking guard kept that
up, he was minutes away from having the damn briefcase wrapped around his neck. "Everyone keeps giving me the bad news. But it's not me you have to

convince, it's the company that chained me to the damn thing.''

"Sounds as if they've been watching too many old cops-and-robbers movies, have they? Either that,'' he added with a sharp look, "or they don't trust you.''

"Don't worry, it's never going to happen again.'' In the interest of peace, Luke ignored the warning dig. "I have a feeling this is going to be my last job. Now, what can I do for you?''

"I'm going to have to get some information from you for the record.'' The guard handed Luke a clipboard and a pen. "Just routine, won't take more than a minute.''

Routine. Like hell. Luke had been around long enough to know the authorities wanted to check his signature against the form he'd filled out to get a license to carry a gun and again when he'd checked it through to Cancún. And just maybe they wanted to pick up a fingerprint or two while they were at it.

Cancún and other faraway places were becoming more attractive by the minute.

He filled in the required lines the man indicated, wincing as he signed his name. He'd used a number of aliases in his career, maybe he should have been using one of them to start with instead of his own name. So much for the anonymity he needed. "Anything else?''

"Nope,'' the man said, carefully pocketing the pen Luke had used. "Merry Christmas!''

"You, too,'' Luke replied in a grim voice as he headed straight for Arden.

Out of the corner of his eye, he caught sight of a

familiar figure, a man he'd worked with recently. The guy had been lurking outside the Majestic back office when the briefcase had been handcuffed to Luke's wrist.

Luke's radar kicked in. Tom Andrews not only knew him, he probably knew what was in the briefcase! What was he doing here? Coincidence? Damn! Something else to worry about.

"Come on," Luke said as he met up with Arden. "I think we have trouble."

Her face paled as he grabbed her arm.

"What kind of trouble?"

"It looks as if Security isn't all that satisfied with our story," he told her as his peripheral vision took in their immediate surroundings.

What he wasn't going to tell her was about his former associate lurking around the terminal…and that Airport Security was still checking on him. She had enough to worry about without that.

"Because of the briefcase?"

"That, and a few other things."

"Like what other things?"

"Just things. If you count the plainclothes detective who's been following us and the security guards who took our names, I'd say we've been under surveillance for a long time."

"What plainclothes detective?" Arden took a quick look around her. "Everyone looks pretty normal to me."

"That's the idea. I'm talking about the guy over there trying to look as if he's holding up that pillar."

''How can you tell he's a detective?'' Arden asked anxiously. ''Maybe you're worrying for nothing.''

''Trust me, I know one when I see one.'' He thought for a few moments. ''Attracting attention by delivering the baby hasn't helped one damn bit!'' he added bitterly.

''What was wrong in helping Jenny Alcott give birth to little Noel?'' Arden questioned. ''It was just like the miracle in the story of Christmas.'' She glanced around the waiting area with a fond smile. ''This might not be a manger, but there is another similarity. We're all travelers without accommodations, aren't we?''

As if that was the only problem! Luke nodded absently. Let her believe in the miracle birth if she wanted to. Anything to make her happy and get her mind off hidden dangers.

He couldn't tell her the things he'd done, the places he'd been, places he'd rather not remember. Nor could he tell her the type of work he'd done since he'd left the government service. Of tracking down wanted criminals and illegal drug traders and other unsavory characters. Of the hazardous and less-than-exotic places he'd traveled to find them. And of the assignments that had taken him into danger. All things that might or might not be on record and could be questioned.

If they were, sure as hell someone wasn't going to take his going south with the briefcase lightly. And especially not after the word got out about what was in it.

''The bad thing is,'' he went on to remind her,

"they're looking for a wanted criminal and his female accomplice. And we fit both descriptions."

Arden's nerves took a turn for the worse. Once again she realized that in less than twenty-four hours she'd gone from being the daughter of a respected minister to a wanted woman!

She may have wanted to prove her independence and to have some adventure in the bargain, but she'd never expected to find herself dodging the law with an unknown stranger, pretending to be his wife!

Not that she'd ever aspired to being a saint, but she hadn't felt like a sinner before this, either.

"I'm sorry to have gotten you into this mess. I should have known better." Luke gazed into her bleak and troubled eyes. She had her own uncertain future to contend with; she didn't need to be involved in his. He should have considered who he was dealing with before he made his impulsive offer to keep her warm.

"Maybe the plane will be cleared to leave before anything else happens," Arden commented hopefully. "The night is almost over."

"Yeah," he agreed, more to reassure her than himself. His life had been full of maybe's, and not all of them had turned out as well as he would have liked.

"Let's go back to the gate and find a place to turn in," he told her. "And don't worry. What's done is done. Maybe we can see ourselves through the rest of the night without any further problems."

He glanced at the colorful holiday gift bag he'd given her. Knowing how she felt about Christmas mornings, maybe its contents would bring a smile to her face.

"You still have Christmas presents to open, you know."

"You mean you want me to open them now instead of waiting for morning?"

"Sure, why not?" Luke answered. "Might as well. There's not much else to do."

Arden wasn't fooled. Luke might speak and act as if he was uninterested, but she sensed there was some part of him that looked forward to Christmas mornings as much as she did. Maybe it had been a time when he was young and before he'd become so cynical and hard. Touched and grateful for the gifts he'd given her, she noted the expectant expression on Luke's face, and it brought a smile to her own.

Maybe opening the gifts would divert them both from their problems. For a little while, at least.

The corner they'd occupied before had been left vacant, almost as if everyone understood that the space belonged to him and Arden.

Agnes Chambers greeted them with a big smile. "You did a great job back there, Mr. McCauley. And you, Mrs. McCauley, I imagine you're very proud of your new husband."

"Yes, indeed," Arden answered with a sidelong glance at Luke. "Very proud." Even though she knew it was all a charade, for these few moments she actually felt like a proud new wife.

Luke acknowledged the congratulations that followed him with a philosophical grin. If he *did* go off to jail, at least he was going to go as a hero.

Arden settled herself, made room for Luke beside

her and drew the first of the three boxes from the gift bag.

"Wait a minute," Luke said, "I'd like to do something first. That is, if you don't mind." He took a pen from his breast pocket, unscrewed it and began numbering the corner of the boxes. "Here, open this one first. After all, it is almost Christmas morning."

Arden unwrapped the box. The little Christmas tree with its fake needles sat there against a backdrop of green wrapping paper. The shop clerk had sprinkled silver confetti over top of the tree and they looked like tiny stars. At its base, the clerk had tucked in white cotton balls to resemble snow.

"There, now you have your own Christmas tree."

"How thoughtful," she said with a wide smile that reminded him of his young sister and of a time when he and the world around him were still innocent. "You were listening to everything I told you, weren't you?"

"Yes," he agreed. *And to some of the things you didn't say,* he thought silently. She may have wanted independence, but as far as he could see, not from the traditional parts of her life that had made her happy. "Go ahead, open the other presents," Luke urged.

The music box was next.

When she unwrapped the red enamel music box, Arden smiled through a sudden blur of happy tears. "How did you know I had a collection of music boxes of my own?"

"I took a wild guess," he answered, fighting back the impulse to wipe her tears away with his fingertips, to taste her smile, to cheer up the young girl that still remained just below the surface of the grown-up Arden. "Maybe you'll be able to have them all back someday. In the meantime, why don't you wind it up?"

"Now? It might disturb someone."

"Now," he said firmly. "It *is* Christmas, isn't it? I'm sure anyone who hears it will enjoy it."

"Rudolph the Red Nosed Reindeer" tinkled through the silence. A harmonica soon softly joined in. The little sleigh started to move across the enameled top. This time Santa raised his arm in a salute.

"How sweet," Arden said, her eyes following the sleigh as it moved across miniature tracks. She gazed up at him with stars in her eyes. "It's the nicest present I've ever been given."

"Ever?" Luke echoed. "It's only a simple little music box, after all. Are you sure you didn't get something more valuable than this somewhere along the line?"

"No, not really," she whispered, holding the music box close to her chest. "This one is special because of the thought behind it."

Luke had shown her a warm heart and a vulnerability behind his cynical facade. He might not want to be told, but he'd given her more than a music box. He'd given her a part of his true self.

She gazed up into his eyes and caught a glimpse of another Luke for a brief moment before it passed from his dark eyes. He might not have wanted her to see his other self, but she had. The profound expression caught at her heart and remained there to be taken out and examined when he was no longer with her. It would give her something to remember him by.

Luke's conscience awakened with a loud bang. If Arden set such great store in a simple music box, would she interpret some special meaning behind the perfume? Perfume was an intimate gift, after all. Usually given by one lover to another. Maybe buying it hadn't been such a good idea.

He wanted to stop her from opening the last box. But he was too late.

Arden was carefully unwrapping the last, small box. She gasped when the tastefully packaged bottle of the White Diamonds perfume came into view.

"Oh, my!" she said, in a voice filled with awe. "Are you sure this is for me?"

"Sure," Luke answered solemnly. "Why not?"

"I've never had perfume before. My folks didn't approve of such things."

"Not even your fiancé?"

"No. It wouldn't have occurred to John to buy some for me. But," she grinned, "sometimes Margo let me use hers. That and a lot of other cosmetics, too. I'd wash them off before I went home."

"So a minister's daughter isn't perfect?"

"Not at all." She gazed down at the bottle of perfume, held it to her nose and turned a wicked grin on him. "I was just as normal as the rest of the girls my age, even if my parents weren't aware of it," she said, turning the elegant box of perfume over and over as if she couldn't believe her eyes. "I'm afraid some of the things Margo talked me into would have sent Mom and Dad over the wall if they'd known what we were doing." Arden grinned. "But, even for a minister's daughter, sometimes it's hard to resist temptation."

Luke knew all about temptation and its various guises. Tonight, he was carrying it in his hand. "Go ahead and open it. After all, your parents aren't here to object," he said wryly. "Enjoy."

"But you've given me so much already!"

"Not really. Let's just say each gift was for a different Arden Crandall."

He saw the questions forming in her eyes. "Maybe I should explain. Let's see." For fear she might misconstrue his intentions, he paused to choose his words carefully. He cared for Arden, perhaps more than he should. But he didn't want her to read too much of a personal nature into the gift.

All he wanted was to put a smile on her face.

"The tree and the music box were for the child in you." he told her.

"And the perfume?"

Their eyes locked. She held her breath.

"The perfume is for the woman."

He couldn't help himself. Not when she gazed at him with her heart in her eyes. He bent over and kissed her on the tip of her nose. Close to the lips he wanted to taste, but as close as he dared to come, considering he was already going too far.

Almost overwhelmed, Arden laid the gifts in her lap. Her heart was filled with gratitude, her mind with questions. Luke was the kind of man a woman dreamed of, but was he the kind to be taken seriously? Or even to consider marrying? As she gazed at him, something in the look he returned told her the gifts were an unspoken goodbye.

Luke saw the questions form in Arden's eyes.

Maybe he'd carried things too far, after all. Maybe she read more into the presents than he actually intended. If so, he was as guilty of taking advantage of her innocence as the other men he worried about.

"I'll remember tonight forever," Arden told him as she started to rewrap her gifts.

Forever echoed in Luke's mind. Who knew better than he that there was no such thing as forever. That forever lasted only as long as time and circumstance allowed. And that sometimes it wasn't as long as the heart wished for.

"Arden," he said reluctantly, "maybe we ought to talk."

Her bright smile as she gave him her full attention almost undid him. But he had to make his intentions clear. She deserved better than to tie up with a man like him.

"Of course," she answered, slowly rewrapping the Christmas tree and the music box. She lingered over the bottle of exotic perfume.

"I'm going to have to trust you to forget everything I told you before and everything I'm going to tell you now. Think you can do that?"

"Yes." Arden dropped her hands in her lap and gave him her full attention.

He took a deep breath. "To start with, tying up with me wasn't the smartest thing you could have done."

"Why not?" Arden's smile disappeared. The troubled look reappeared. "I'm afraid I don't understand. You did tell me you weren't a wanted man. Or are you?"

He wanted to take her hands. To shield her from the truth, but he didn't dare.

He hated himself for what he was about to do.

"No, I'm not. Not in the way you think. What I'm trying to tell you..." His voice dropped. He couldn't bring himself to tell her the whole truth about himself, but he had to tell her just enough to make her forget him. "I don't know how else to say it—but I'm not exactly the type of man you met at church."

Arden's eyes lightened. "I knew that right away," she confessed with a smile. "To tell you the truth, I'd had enough of saintly men." A wicked grin came over her face. "I don't think I would have taken you up on your offer if you had been."

Luke shook his head. He didn't wanted her to take his confession lightly. On the other hand, he didn't want to frighten her, either. Maybe somewhere in between.

"I haven't been the kind of a guy you should want to know. No," he said over her protests, "it's true. In fact," he said with a wry grin, "you might say I've been the kind of man your father warned you against."

"My father has nothing to do with this," Arden answered. "He doesn't know you. For that matter, maybe I don't know too much about you, either. But what I do know tells me you aren't the man you seem to be on the surface."

She knew better than he what her eyes had seen and what her heart was telling her.

"I'm afraid you haven't been around me enough to recognize what's beneath the surface," he said adamantly. "Frankly, I'm a man who's seen and done too

much. Things you wouldn't dream of. Out of a sense
of duty to my country, sure. But, I have to admit, it
was also the danger that drew me." He grimaced.
"Maybe I just wasn't smart enough to stay out of trouble.
And the few times I tried, it caught up with me,
anyway."

"Me, too," Arden replied. "Take my meeting up
with my aunt and uncle, for instance."

Luke had to smile. "It's not exactly the same thing,
Arden."

Her eyes seemed to take on a shine as she listened
to him. With a sinking heart, he knew that although
he'd been trying to discourage her fantasies, he'd actually
encouraged them!

He took her hands in his. "Now, look, Arden. I'm
trying to tell you I've had enough danger and excitement
to last me for the rest of my life. I want out.
Maybe that's what you're looking for, I don't know.
And if you're looking for freedom and independence,
so am I. Even if it's for different reasons and not in
the same way."

"So far you haven't said anything I can't live
with," she answered.

"That's the point," he answered gently. "I don't
want you to have to live with it."

He couldn't afford to fall in love. Not with any
woman and definitely not with Arden. Not without
giving up the plans he'd made to take him into his
future. He *was* being honest. At least, about that. And
he didn't want to be the cause of turning Arden into
a dishonest woman.

For Arden's sake, and his own, he hardened his heart.

"This whole thing between us started as an impulse on my part. It's time to stop before it goes too far."

Actually, under different circumstances, Luke would have felt perhaps that things hadn't gone far enough. But he had to live with himself.

Arden felt herself color as she considered what Luke was telling her. He sounded as if he thought she'd wanted an affair when they reached Cancún! Had she been so naive about the way she was beginning to feel about him? Was she so transparent? Had she actually shown the attraction she'd felt and still felt for him?

Nothing in her upbringing had prepared her for even the thought of an affair. And nothing had actually been farther from her mind. But she *had* been attracted to him. At this point she wasn't sure just what it was she *did* want.

To her, Luke had been a decent, warm and caring man who had treated her as a grown man treats a grown woman. And she felt she'd responded to him the same way.

A small inner voice sounded, chiding her, reminding her of the truth. She was calling the feeling between them attraction, but was the attraction actually the first stages of romantic love?

Impossible! It wasn't as if they'd shared a lifetime of common experiences; they'd actually met less than twelve hours ago. No matter how she felt about him, they were strangers.

He wanted his independence, his freedom to go his own way. To live a dream. So did she.

How could she have fallen in love with Luke without giving up the small measure of independence it had taken her twenty-two years to get up enough courage to carve out for herself?

Chapter Nine

Luke was right. It was time to say goodbye.

They'd been strangers when they met and would be strangers when they parted in the morning. There was no point in indulging in her fantasy that he could be Mr. Right when he was so obviously Mr. Wrong. He had his reasons for wanting to go his own way, but then didn't she? Or had she forgotten her desire for independence so soon?

"Of course," she answered. She schooled her expression carefully so that Luke wouldn't see her inner struggle. "Maybe we can have breakfast together in Cancún before you leave?"

Luke breathed a sigh of relief. Arden hadn't forgotten he'd told her he was going to catch the charter plane's return flight to New York. So far, things had gone better than he'd hoped for.

He couldn't tell her he had no intention of showing up at the Majestic Hotel Resort after the plane landed. And that when he disappeared, he would take the contents of the briefcase with him.

Gazing at the studied smile on Arden's face, he

could see hurt in her eyes no matter how she tried to hide it. He felt as though he'd betrayed her.

"Great, I'm looking forward to it." Even as he told the lie a hollow feeling came over him at the thought of never seeing Arden again.

"McCauley! Hey, wait up a minute!"

Luke groaned as eyes and ears turned in his direction. He turned back to see Larry Alcott barreling toward them. "What are you doing here? I thought you went along to the hospital with your wife and baby?"

"I did," the new father said, wearing a proud grin. "I came back here to get our things, when the doctors advised me to let Jenny and the baby rest for a day or two before I take them home. I was too excited to think of taking our things with us before."

He peered around the holding area. "This doesn't look like the same gate where Noel was born."

"I know," Luke agreed with a weary shrug. "We've been kept on the move so often I don't recognize it myself anymore."

"You don't happen to have any of our carry-on luggage with you, do you?"

"No, and not our own, either. I'm afraid we've learned the hard way never to leave luggage unattended. Hope yours didn't have anything of value."

"Just our tour documents and some extra clothing." Alcott shrugged his shoulders. "I don't suppose anyone can use the documents, anyway. Not with Ms. Chambers standing guard. As for the clothes, I don't think Jenny will mind losing them. She's too happy with the baby to complain about a little thing like that."

"Too bad about the honeymoon," Luke offered as he shook Alcott's offered hand. "Maybe you can celebrate later."

"Oh, sure." Alcott looked sheepish but obviously too happy at being a new father to mind missing a honeymoon. "It's going to have to wait a few months until the baby is old enough to take along."

"How's the kid doing?"

"He's fine," Alcott beamed his pride in his new son. "In fact, he's the best Christmas present Jenny and I've ever received. Thanks to you."

"I didn't have much to do with it," Luke answered dryly. "I just tried to make your wife comfortable. Nature did the rest."

"Nah, you're just being modest. You talked her through the birth when it should have been me helping, just like in the Lamaze classes we took," Alcott answered. "But I'm afraid it got too much for me. Maybe we can do something for you some day. In fact, I kinda wish you would have let us name the baby after you."

Luke smiled, thinking of the unwanted notoriety already attached to him and of things to come. And what Alcott's reaction would be if he knew the truth about what Luke was contemplating.

"Just look at it this way," he advised. "You did the kid a favor when you named him Noel."

"If you think so. But we won't forget you—ever." Alcott offered his hand for a final handshake. "Well, I have to get back. You did a wonderful job with my wife and son last night." He beamed at Arden. "You did, too. I don't know how to thank you both."

"Just glad we could help," Luke answered. He was uncomfortable with all the praise being heaped on him. Besides, he thought with a shudder, of the two births he'd witnessed, the Alcott blessed event had been a whole lot easier on him.

"Say, what's the weather like outside?" Luke asked, anxious to get the subject off himself. "Any chance of the storm letting up anytime soon?"

"Yeah, a little, maybe. It's not snowing right now, but it's still cold and icy as hell." He caught himself. "Sorry for the language, Mrs. McCauley. It's just that I slipped half a dozen times getting from the taxi to the terminal. Well, so long! And Merry Christmas to you both."

"Something good came out of the storm, didn't it?" Arden said as she watched Alcott disappear into the crowd.

Luke turned back to gaze at the wistful smile on her face. A smile that cracked the hard shell around his doubting heart. "I couldn't agree more," he answered. *But it wasn't only because of the miracle of tiny Noel's birth.* He'd found Arden, hadn't he? Even if only for a little while.

Maybe if they'd met at an earlier time in his life things might have ended differently. Before he'd become so hard, so cynical. And before he'd decided to enjoy the rest of his life in a manner that wasn't exactly socially acceptable.

He was searching for a clear place to settle down for the night when he heard his name called again.

"Hey, McCauley!"

This time, the low-pitched sinister call stirred

Luke's memory of bygone threats. He'd been the target of dozens of disgruntled felons during his career with the government agency and this was one of them. But this was a voice he would have preferred never to have heard again.

Instinctively he started to reach for his gun and stepped in front of Arden to shield her. Damn! The gun was somewhere in the bowels of the Majestic plane! All of his senses went on alert. He turned to meet the eyes of a short, stocky dark-haired man who stood regarding him. The man's menacing stance and the angry expression on his face was enough to send chills down Luke's spine.

Joe Hoyt was a desperate man out of his past. A man he'd brought in for trial three years ago and who'd sworn to pay him back someday. A man who, the last Luke had heard, was in prison serving a twenty-to-life sentence for peddling drugs on the barrio streets of Chicago.

"What are *you* doing here?" Luke's eyes scrutinized Hoyt's clothing for any suspicious bulge that might broadcast the presence of a weapon.

"Meeting a friend, if it's any of your business," Hoyt sneered. "I'm out on appeal, no thanks to you. Got myself a good lawyer this time."

Meeting someone with a supply of drugs, more likely, Luke thought, but it wasn't his business anymore. "Your lawyer's not going to be good enough to keep you out of prison. I predict you'll be back in no time," Luke answered. "The law is the law. I don't know anyone who's bent it in more places than you."

"Oh, yeah, wise guy?" Hoyt's face grew mottled

with his anger, his fists clenched and unclenched as he glared at Luke. "You think you're so damn smart. Hell, guys like you have had everything go your way all your life. You don't know what guys like me have to do just to stay alive."

"Maybe. But ruining other people's lives by selling them drugs isn't the answer," Luke answered darkly.

"For all the good it's going to do you, keep preaching." The drug dealer's feral grin was as crooked as his teeth. "The word's out on you, sucker. Your day's coming. And sooner than you think."

Icy fingers ran up and down Luke's spine. He squared his shoulders and looked Hoyt directly in the eyes. In the man's angry dark eyes, Luke's worst nightmare stared back at him. He'd been in danger before, but this time things were different. He couldn't rely on an official background to keep the guy in check or to bring him in. And with plans of his own, he couldn't afford to take the chance on calling in terminal authorities.

He'd never been afraid before, and he wasn't now. Not for himself. But he was afraid for Arden's safety, now that Hoyt was eyeing what he could see of her with more than a little interest.

He inventoried his chances of protecting her from the street scum who was looking at her in such a predatory way. With the briefcase chained to his wrist and his holster empty, there was little he could do to defend her.

"Your woman?" Hoyt asked with a look of avarice on his swarthy face.

"None of your damn business," Luke answered. He

could feel Arden come to life behind him. From past experience, he knew she was gutsy enough to come up front and give Hoyt the dressing down of his life if he didn't stop her. He shot a quick warning look behind him and prayed she wouldn't do anything foolish.

"If you have anything more to say, spit it out," he told Hoyt. "Otherwise, I suggest you get lost."

"What's the matter, scared?"

Luke had had enough. He was sorely tempted to teach the guy a lesson he'd never forget. Or to strangle the bastard with the chain dangling from his wrist. But it was the wrong time for teaching Hoyt a lesson. There was Arden to consider.

"Not of you, punk," he replied. "I'm busy right now. But, pick the time and the place and I'll show you how scared I am."

Hoyt laughed. "Hell, not with all these people around. I ain't as stupid as that. If I was you, I'd watch my back. I'm going to take care of you when you least expect it," he sneered. "And I won't be sending you my calling card when I'm ready."

Hoyt craned his neck trying to catch a glimpse of Arden. "So long, lady. Better enjoy your copper while you can."

A hollow pit in his stomach, Luke watched the man swagger away. If he felt as if his blood had turned to ice, he wondered how a woman sheltered from this side of life would react. The low snort of contempt behind him told him what Arden thought of the deadly scene she witnessed. Instead of being afraid, she sounded angry enough to join the argument.

What would she do if she were on her own and something like this happened to her?

Any thought of leaving her on her own evaporated in the cold wind that suddenly seemed to blow through the terminal.

"Why don't you turn that man over to the authorities?" Arden demanded as she came out from behind him. "Or at least let me tell him what I thought of him!"

"Stay out of it, Arden." Luke advised her. "You don't know what you're up against with a man like Hoyt."

Luke watched Hoyt disappear in the crowd and mulled over the possibilities facing him. He could turn him in to the airport authorities, except it was likely the guy probably was legitimately out on bail or he wouldn't have been so willing to be conspicuous. Besides, Hoyt hadn't done anything illegal, not this time, anyway. The guy was at the airport for some reason, and Luke doubted it was to welcome someone home.

It was his word against Hoyt's, and with suspicion already cast Luke's way, he knew the answer to that one.

Was the presence of his former associate, Tom Andrews, and Hoyt's appearance merely coincidence? Luke had the gut feeling Andrews knew what was in the briefcase and wanted it for himself. Coupled with knowing Hoyt had a score to settle, one and one added up to two shady characters. What if they'd somehow gotten together?

It was no use calling in the authorities. With his

luck, he'd wind up having to take a trip downtown to the nearest police precinct.

Luke knew Hoyt was right. He'd be smart to watch his back.

But first he had to find some way to get Arden out of sight, to protect her from trouble until the storm passed and flights were called. Until then, there was safety in numbers.

If only Arden wasn't wearing that too-wide, too-long white sweatshirt that broadcast I Love NY in letters that seemed to be a foot tall and calling attention to her.

"Come on," he said, putting his free arm around Arden's shoulders. "Everything's going to be okay. Those were nothing more than empty threats of a desperate man. Unless he can find a judge who's lost his marbles, the guy's going to be back in prison before he knows what hit him."

But he knew from experience there were judges who could be bought.

"It sounded as though he intends to get even with you for what he says you did to him." Arden shuddered. "And to get even with me when he doesn't even know me! You should have let me talk some sense into him."

"Over my dead body," Luke replied grimly. "I doubt that even your father could straighten the guy out."

There was some comfort in the thought that Arden would be safely out of the guy's reach after tomorrow. And, if things went as he'd planned, so would he.

Something else was bothering him. The knowledge

he was contemplating doing something to betray Arden's trust in him. After tonight, it was beginning to bother the hell out of him.

He eyed her uneasily. Unless he missed his guess, this was the first time she'd come face-to-face with real trouble. Nothing in her background would have prepared her for tonight's unexpected scenario.

"Let's go back and join the tour group," he said. "I could use a little company about now."

Arden regarded Luke out of the corner of her eye. The dark and dangerous edge to him had returned, stronger than in the romantic fantasy she'd woven around him. That he might be involved in life-threatening circumstances like the one she'd just witnessed hadn't occurred to her until now. And that she might become involved in it herself was something she'd never thought of, either.

"Maybe you ought to report the man?" she asked uneasily. "What if he comes back?"

"I thought about that, but you can't arrest a man for making threats," Luke answered. "Hoyt wouldn't dare do anything with so many people around, and not before his new hearing, anyway. We'll be long gone by then."

"You're sure?"

"I'm sure. Besides, he thinks you're my wife. He wouldn't be looking for an Arden Crandall."

Except that too many people knew her as Arden McCauley.

"In that case, do you suppose we could find something to eat," Arden commented, gazing wistfully around her. "I don't know when I've been so hungry."

Luke hated to leave her long enough to check out the food concessions. On the other hand, it *would* take her mind off Hoyt.

He studied the waiting area for a familiar face. There were none, but he had the uneasy feeling he hadn't heard the last from Hoyt, or possibly Andrews.

"Wait over there in the corner and don't talk to anyone. I'll make a quick foray and try to find something. If you see anything suspicious, holler for Security and scream your head off. I'll be back in a few minutes."

Arden watched him go with a sad smile. Instead of her being turned off by the Hoyt incident, she felt a stronger attraction for Luke than ever. He was still the man of her fantasies, and larger than life.

"Pardon me, Mrs. McCauley! Mrs. McCauley?"

Unused to being called by that name, it took Arden a minute to realize she was being called. She turned around. It was the security guard with the Man-Wanted poster in his hand. "Yes?"

"I'm sorry to bother you again, but I just can't put your husband out of my mind. The resemblance between him and this guy keeps bugging me. As far as I can tell, the only difference between them is the mustache."

"So?"

"So, did you ever see your husband with a mustache?"

Arden hid a shiver. The man's resemblance to Luke *was* enough to make anyone question it.

Who *was* Luke, anyway? The bank robber with a phony passport or the former lawman he claimed to be? There *was* that briefcase...

"I can assure you, my husband is not the man in the poster!" she said emphatically. Luke had already struck a chord within her that no amount of suspicions could change. Not until he confessed to being a criminal.

"And you're not his accomplice, either," he answered with a leer. "So you said."

"Right," Arden answered, putting the steel in her voice she remembered her father had used on her when there had been no room for argument. "And as a matter of fact, your questions are becoming annoying! Why can't you just leave us alone?"

"Just doing my job, Mrs. McCauley, just doing my job," the man answered. "Say, how long did you say you knew your husband before you married him?"

"I didn't say. But it was long enough."

"I'd still like to have a few words with him," the guard insisted. "Where is he by the way?"

"Trying to find me something to eat."

"Really? Considering that the cupboards are bare around here, I'd say he's off on a fool's errand. Or maybe—" he paused with a sly emphasis that made Arden's skin crawl "—he's taken this opportunity to get away. If he's the guy in the poster, maybe he's run out on you."

Run out on her? Never! Arden felt she knew Luke better than that. He'd never leave her alone after Hoyt had threatened them.

"You don't know my husband or you wouldn't suggest such a thing.'' She glared at him sternly, daring him to make the next move. She knew the law well enough to know he couldn't arrest her without cause. And so far, her only misstep had been to abandon her luggage. Unless, of course, she realized with an inward shudder, linking up with Luke turned out to be a crime.

''Okay, for now,'' the man said. ''But this isn't over until it's over. The heist your husband was involved in resulted in a bank security officer getting killed. We take care of our own.'' He put the Wanted poster back in his breast pocket.

Her husband.

In her mind, Arden *became* Luke's wife. She took care of her own, too, she thought grimly as she watched the guard stride away.

''What did he want?'' Luke asked as he came back.

''Just the same old subject. He wanted to know if you're the man in the Wanted poster,'' Arden replied. ''I told him he was wrong.''

''He is,'' Luke said quietly, gazing into Arden's eyes. ''You have my word on it.''

He wanted to take her in his arms and show her how grateful he was for her loyalty and how much she was beginning to mean to him. But he couldn't. Not after he'd already said goodbye.

''We're in luck,'' he told her. ''One of the bakeries decided to make an early delivery in between snow flurries.'' He held up a plastic baggie with a croissant and a Danish inside. ''It cost a bundle, but you won't go hungry, after all.''

"How much is a bundle?" Arden asked curiously as she reached for the croissant. "I can pay my share."

"Too much," Luke answered as he remembered it had cost him his last twenty. "But it was worth every penny."

And it was, he thought, as he saw Arden bite into the croissant and her eyes light up in pleasure. He might be broke for now, but barring any unforeseen problems, there *was* that pot of gold waiting for him.

He was about to bite into the pastry when he heard an ominous conversation beside him.

"I don't care! Sitting on the floor in an airport terminal isn't my idea of a honeymoon." A sobbing bride cried into her groom's shoulder. "I want to go home!"

"Aw, honey," her husband said as he tried to comfort her. "It's not so bad. The hard part's behind us. It'll be morning before you know it. We're bound to be on our way as soon as the sun comes up."

"I don't believe you. My back is killing me and I have an upset stomach."

Luke snapped to attention and peered around him. Another pregnant bride?

His gaze met the beleaguered groom's eyes in time to see recognition dawn.

"I'm sure you're going to be fine. It's just been too much excitement for you," the man told his new wife. "Besides, I've just noticed someone right here beside you who can take care of you if you need him."

"I don't care who's here! I want to lie down in a decent bed!"

Luke exchanged glances with Arden. He curbed an

impulse to grab her and run. He wasn't a doctor, and he didn't intend to play at being one. Not again.

"Arden," he whispered quietly. "I think we'd better move on."

"I'm sorry," she answered sleepily. "I don't think I can move another muscle even if I had to."

"Maybe so, but it sounds as if there's some kind of trouble with the bride on my right. I don't intend to get involved this time. I don't even want to be asked to put a Band-Aid on someone's finger."

A tense, male voice sounded in Luke's ear. "Say, aren't you the guy who delivered a baby a few hours ago?"

Luke turned back and reluctantly nodded his agreement. "I'm afraid that was me. Why?"

"My name is Henry Gaithers, and this is my wife, Cindy. I've got to find out when the plane is leaving for Cancún. If ours isn't going to leave soon, I'm going to have to find a place where my wife can lie down. It's either that or take her home and catch another plane some other time. We'd hate to miss our honeymoon."

Luke glanced at the teary Cindy Gaithers. Just what that bit of news had to do with him, he didn't know. And he wasn't in a hurry to find out.

"So, I was wondering if you could keep an eye on my wife until I get back?"

"I'm not a doctor, you know," Luke replied reluctantly. "I don't know what I could do for her. Maybe you ought to take her home?"

Arden poked him in the ribs. Her message was clear.

"Okay," Luke said wearily. "We'll be glad to keep Mrs. Gaithers company."

"Great! Cindy, Mr. McCauley and his wife are going to stay with you while I'm gone. I'll be right back."

Arden moved to sit beside the teary bride. She took her hands in her own. "It's just wedding jitters, Cindy. You're coming down from a high. Take it from me, you're going to be fine."

"Are you sure?" Cindy said doubtfully, rubbing her moist forehead. "I feel terrible!"

"Yes," Arden answered with a rueful smile. Nothing could come close to her own jitters that had prompted her to run from her wedding. "I remember my own. I was a basket case for a while." Her eyes locked with Luke's. "But everything turned out better than I expected. And it will for you, too."

Cindy Gaithers eyed her up and down. "Say, aren't you the one whose luggage was stolen earlier tonight?"

"I'm afraid so," Arden said ruefully. She glanced down at herself. "What I have on is all I own until I can get to Cancún."

Arden's comments dried Cindy's tears. "Gee, that's too bad. Maybe I can lend you a few things."

"No, thanks. Don't worry about me. What I need is a hot shower and I'll be fine."

"Got it, sweetheart!"

Henry Gaithers barreled back into sight waving a key.

"Got what?" his wife asked. "It had better be good, Henry Gaithers, or I'm going home!"

"The key to a roomette!"

Cindy Gaithers peered at the key. "A roomette? What's a roomette?"

"It's a small comfort room over on the international side of the airport for travelers to freshen up between flights."

She seemed to digest that information for a while. "Has it got a bed?"

"Yes. Well, maybe," he said as an afterthought. "Sort of a bed. Actually it's more like a cot. But it has a toilet and a shower."

Luke perked up. He'd rented a roomette himself on occasion when he had to wait between flights. If they were available, maybe he could latch on to one for Arden and get her out of sight for the rest of the night.

On second thought, he wondered, how in blazes had the man been able to rent one when the entire terminal was bulging with stranded passengers?

"How did you manage to find an empty roomette on a night like this?" he asked.

"Well," Gaithers said proudly, "I bought the key off a guy waiting for a flight to the Orient. He's been hanging around for two days. Told me he got fed up hanging around and decided to go back home and wait out the storm in comfort."

"Why didn't he use the roomette?" his wife asked.

"He said he bought it off someone else before he took a good look at it. When he did, he decided it was too small for him to stay in overnight. Seems the guy has claustrophobia."

"Claustrophobia?" his wife gasped. "You know darn well I have the same phobia!"

"I know, sweetheart, but under the circumstances, I thought you might put up with the small size of the room. It'll only be for a little while."

"No, thank you!" With an apologetic glance at Arden, Cindy started to gather up her belongings.

"Come on, Cindy. It cost me a lot of money to get the roomette for you. I can't let it go to waste!"

His wife's eyes narrowed. "How much is a lot of money?"

"Well… All I had with me. Two hundred and fifty dollars, if you must know. The guy wouldn't take a check."

"That was our honeymoon money! What are we going to do without it?"

"Now, sweetheart, take it easy. I did it for you. I figured I could wire my boss back here and get a loan on next month's salary. After all, you were the one who wanted to get married now and have a honeymoon. I liked things just fine the way we were."

His wife's face turned the color of a red brick. "Henry Gaithers, how could you embarrass me this way! Now everyone will know we've been living together."

"Take it easy, honey. Lots of people live together before their wedding day. Why don't you look at it this way. At least we're married now."

Luke could see from the look on Cindy Gaithers' face that it was the wrong thing to say.

She struggled to her feet. "I'm going home—with or without you!"

"How about the money I paid for the roomette?" her husband protested.

"I'll buy it from you for the two hundred and fifty," a voice shouted.

Luke became aware they were suddenly surrounded by interested spectators.

"I'll make it three hundred!" another voice shouted. "Hell, we don't even know if the airport will open in the morning!"

"Four hundred!"

"Four hundred and fifty!"

"Five hundred," Luke heard himself shout above the tumult. "I'll give you five hundred for the key!"

"Done," Gaithers said. There was a howl of protests. "After all," he explained to the other clamoring bidders, "this man did me a favor when I needed him. I owed him one."

Luke was in a state of shock. He didn't have five hundred dollars on him—not anymore! But somehow the idea of a room—private, secure, that he could go to with Arden—carried him away. Before he could think rationally about the sum he was bidding, he was the owner of a roomette. "Will you take a check?" he asked.

"Sure," Gaithers answered, "but only because it's you. A favor in return for a favor is the way I see it."

A favor in return for a favor? Luke had trouble keeping his face impassive. Hell, the guy had doubled his money in the space of a few minutes. What kind of favor was that?

Luke pulled out his wallet and reluctantly took out the spare check he kept folded there for emergencies. He'd had no business getting involved in the bidding in the first place. But as long as he was in this deep, he'd do the right thing.

"What are you doing?" Arden whispered.

"Making sure you're going to be safe, comfortable and out of sight until the airport reopens."

She smiled at him, the surprise and gratitude clearly on her face. "Thank you," she said simply, and Luke felt it all the way to his toes. There was something about this woman—an innocence, and a sensuality simmering underneath it—that got to him. And no matter how many times he told himself to ignore her, to bide his time with her now and say goodbye to her later, he wasn't able.

"Before we go," she asked him, a glint in her suddenly sparkling eyes, "I have one question."

"And what's that?"

She suddenly looked demure. "Are—are you going to share the room with me?"

Luke didn't have to think twice.

Chapter Ten

Arden stepped up to Gaithers. "Will you take my traveler's checks?"

Before Gaithers could reply, Luke roared, "What are you doing? I'll pay for it."

"Put back your wallet," she whispered as she put her hand over his. "I can pay my own way. Besides, I have the feeling you'd rather not leave a personal check behind you." At his nod, she started to hand the checks over.

"Wait a minute, Henry," Cindy Gaithers broke in excitedly as her husband reached for the checks. "We have to take care of something first."

"What's wrong?" Her husband glanced wearily at his wife.

"Arden doesn't have any luggage!"

"My bags were stolen last night," Arden said, waving the checks. "But luckily I had these checks with me in my purse."

"Sure, but it still means you have nothing to wear tonight except what you have on," Cindy said with a grin as she gestured to the I Love NY sweatshirt. "That's no way to start a honeymoon. Anyway, if you're going to spend your wedding night in a tiny roomette, you'll want to change into some fresh clothes in the morning.''

"That would be great, except that I don't see how I could manage that. All I own is what I have on," Arden said wistfully, glancing down at the rumpled shirt. Large enough to fit a football quarterback, it hung down to her knees and, even rolled at the wrists, the sleeves hung over her hands.

"I have a great idea," Cindy announced. As the crowd around them grew larger, drawn by Cindy's exclamation, she gestured at the brides among the curious bystanders. "I'll bet we could all chip in and give you a bridal shower!"

A bridal shower? In an airport?

Arden thought wistfully of the contrast between the bridal shower Margo had given her three weeks ago and the one Cindy was suggesting take place in a snowbound airport.

Margo's party had been held in a scrumptious hotel dining room hung with fresh holly, where the scent of gaily decorated Christmas fir trees had filled the air. Each tree had had a different motif, from simple lights and colored bulbs to one that depicted the story of Hansel and Gretel with tiny gingerbread cottages strung throughout its branches. Colorfully wrapped boxes had been piled on mounds of fake snow packed beneath the trees.

The high tea, featuring gourmet teas from around the world had been served on lace-covered tables. Tea cakes and delicate sandwiches of paté and cucumbers on silver platters had been presented by waitresses in exotic costumes. A violin and a flute had played sentimental love songs in the background while she'd unwrapped intimate bridal lingerie to Margo's ribald comments and bursts of laughter.

Arden shuddered at the reminder that there were unwrapped wedding gifts at home, waiting for her return from her honeymoon. Her mother would have to make excuses and return gifts, instead of the expected thank-you notes. Excuses that made little sense to anyone but Arden.

Instead of dreamy violin music, the only sounds surrounding her were coming from the stranded, half-awake members of the Honeymoon Express Tour. As for food service, the chances of Cindy finding something fit for a celebration like a bridal shower were slim to none.

And yet tonight here was Cindy Gaithers cheerfully proposing a bridal shower in the holding area of a cold, dimly lit airport terminal. And where the guests would all be strangers.

Poised like a cheerleader, Cindy waved her arms and called to the brides in the crowd that surrounded them. "Come on, girls, let's give Arden a bridal shower! What do you say?"

"A shower?" her husband asked, looking longingly at Arden's packet of traveler's checks. "Come on, honey, let's just take the checks and leave. This whole thing started when you said you wanted to go home and get off your feet!"

"I do, but things have changed. We can go home later. This is going to be fun!" Cindy patted his shoulder. "Besides, Arden was so nice to me while you were gone, the least I can do for her is to return the favor. Just like you're doing for her husband, sweetheart.'' She turned back to the spectators. ''Arden McCauley doesn't even have a toothbrush to start off her honeymoon! We women have to stick together, don't we?''

''Yes indeed!'' The tour leader, Agnes Chambers, cheerfully agreed. ''If we can hold a wedding reception here, there's no reason why we can't have a bridal shower! Besides, it'll help pass the time. In fact, I'd like to be the one to give Arden her first shower gift.''

She dug in her voluminous carpetbag and came up with a small, blue drawstring bag labeled Comfort Kit. Courtesy of Majestic Airlines. ''There, now you have a toothbrush,'' she announced with a flourish, ''and toothpaste, a comb and a small washcloth.''

A clamor of questions about what would be an appropriate gift went up as Cindy efficiently went about organizing the bridal shower.

''Now, each of you dig in your overnight bags and see if there's anything you can spare. Arden can buy anything else she needs in Cancún, but we want her honeymoon to start off right, don't we?''

''I'm game,'' a male voice inquired. ''Who has some champagne left? I don't have a present, but I don't mind drinking to the bride.''

''Cut it out, Rudy! This isn't a wedding reception. This is a bridal shower. Men aren't invited!''

''Why not?'' her husband asked. ''A party's a party!''

''Because a bridal shower is a girl thing, that's why.''

"Let him stay," Cindy interjected. "We want to give Arden a good send-off."

"Then, how about some music for dancing? Let's make this a real party."

"Hold up for a minute. First things first," Cindy interjected. "What else do any of you have extra that we can give Arden?"

"I've got an extra hairbrush I can give her," one bride announced. "And some of my special lily of the valley shampoo."

"And I have the bobby socks and slippers I was going to wear on the plane to give my feet a rest from these new shoes!"

"You can borrow my new negligee," a new feminine voice broke in, "but I'd like to have it back when we get to Cancún!"

"Are you sure you want to do that, honey?" a male voice questioned anxiously. "I was kinda looking forward to seeing you in it, you know."

"Hush, Peter!" his bride blushed and announced in a stage whisper. "You're embarrassing me. There'll be plenty of time for that later. I'm only trying to help poor Arden get properly started on her honeymoon. After what happened to her, she needs a break."

Arden blushed when everyone's eyes, bright with speculation, turned on her. She remembered Margo's gift, a sheer white nightgown and negligee ensemble, that had been stolen along with her luggage. The thought ignited a heated response through her middle as she recalled the note Margo had slipped inside the gift box. It had given Arden tongue-in-cheek tips on how to handle what she'd dubbed THE GREAT AWAKENING.

Husband or not, THE GREAT AWAKENING had troubled Arden when she connected it with her former fiancé. She was glad he was out of the picture. Not that she intended tonight to be *the* night either, but the thought of Luke's mysterious and intriguing aura made THE GREAT AWAKENING seem different. A wedding night surely wouldn't be all that an unwelcome experience with a man like him.

For the first time, she dared to contemplate spending the night ahead with Luke in the terms Margo's notes had suggested.

On the other hand, she had no business thinking of Margo's hints at all at a time like this, and especially in connection with Luke. They weren't really married, and tonight wasn't their wedding night. For Pete's sake, they'd only met a few hours ago! How did she know he was willing?

She had no business contemplating THE AWAKENING with the first truly appealing man she met. Even with as interesting and mysterious a man as Luke. Especially when he'd already said goodbye.

But, to her chagrin, somehow she was!

"Now, who has a dress for Arden to wear in the morning?"

A buzz went around the group. It was clear no one had an extra dress in their overnight bags. And that the bulk of their clothing was in their luggage on the Majestic charter plane.

"Oh, well," Cindy decided as she looked down at

the small pile of gifts in her hands. "I guess Arden doesn't need a dress. Not tonight, anyway."

At the renewed giggles and knowing looks, Arden wondered if Luke was aware her blood had turned to molten lava. The last thing she wanted him to know, considering her wandering thoughts. "Cindy, please!" she whispered.

"Well, here you go," Cindy said as she handed the gifts to Arden. "There's enough stuff here to get you started. At least for your wedding night, anyway."

In the dim recess of her mind, Arden heard her father's voice thundering she was headed straight for the road to hell if she left her wedding. Judging from the speculative looks everyone was giving her, and the thoughts of the forbidden fruits of desire that tempted her, she was ready to believe she was well on her way.

Especially now that she'd let everyone believe she was Luke's wife when she wasn't his wife at all.

"I'll donate another flight bag to carry all of the gifts you ladies were nice enough to give Mrs. McCauley," the tour leader said. "Here you go!" She helped Arden put the gifts inside the bag.

"Say, wait a minute! I just thought of something you can use for underwear in the morning!" Cindy Gaithers reached for her overnight bag, drew out a brief red and white two piece string bikini and waved it in the air.

"Underwear?" Her heart caught as Arden caught a glimpse of the frankly assessing look on Luke's face. How could she put on a string bikini if his mind was wandering down on the same tempting paths as hers were taking?

More to the point, how could she stay out of trouble when her senses were responding to that look? Especially if they were going to spend the rest of the night together in the tiny roomette.

"Sure," Cindy assured her. "It's better than nothing. If you're lucky enough to have a shower in that room, like Henry said, it will give you a chance to shower and change into something comfortable and fresh. Too bad we couldn't find a dress for you."

"Thank you." Arden cringed as a dozen interested male eyes studied the bikini then swiveled back to her. Why did her wedding night have to be so public?

"Sure, I won't need it where I'm going," Cindy assured her with a wink and an inviting glance at her husband. "When I get home, Henry and I are going straight to bed."

Arden felt herself flush as she pictured herself wearing the too-brief garment. Avoiding Luke's eyes, she hurriedly rolled the bikini into a small ball and stuffed it into her new flight bag. The charade of masquerading as Mrs. McCauley and being left alone with him in confined quarters loomed larger than life.

A bikini! Luke blinked. How was he going to get through the rest of the night with the picture in his mind of Arden wearing the two mere slips of silk that didn't look as if they were large enough to cover a Barbie doll. Or if she chose to wear the donated nightgown that didn't leave much to the imagination either.

On the other hand, things were really beginning to get interesting. He watched as other brides gathered around Arden and chipped in their advice on how she should go about her wedding night. He hid his amusement at the chagrined look on Arden's face. What must the naive Arden be thinking now?

He felt sorry for her. Enough was enough. As her husband, he felt it was time to put an end to the shower. He made his way to her side and took her by her arm. "Time to go, if we're going to get any rest at all."

Cindy Gaithers burst into laughter. "Rest! Who's kidding whom?"

"Hey, wait a minute!" Henry Gaithers elbowed his way through the chattering brides. "Maybe you ought to sign those traveler's checks before you forget."

Taking care to speak softly into her ear so no one could overhear, Luke slid a protective arm around Arden. "Are you sure you want to do this? I'm still willing to give the man my check."

"Yes, I know you are, and I appreciate it," she answered. "But it's time for me to start taking care of myself." She rummaged inside her purse for a pen. "I'll need a flat surface so I can endorse these checks."

"Use my shoulders," Gaithers said hurriedly as he turned his back. "The sooner we get this over with, the sooner Cindy and I can get home to bed."

"And so can the McCauleys," Cindy interjected.

Cindy laughed. Someone whistled. Arden blushed.

Luke gave in. Arden was right. It looked as if she would have to take care of herself after tonight. She may not have paid attention to everything he'd told her about himself, but it was obvious she'd heard the goodbye in his voice. It was just as well.

He'd hated to have to say goodbye to her the first

time; he didn't know how he could bring himself to say it again. Not when he wanted so much to take her in his arms as a real husband would.

"Arden Crandall, I knew I would find you in the center of all this excitement!"

The crowd parted as Jane Peterson bustled up to her niece.

"Arthur," she called over her shoulder, "I told you Arden would be behind this, didn't I?"

Breathless from following in his wife's wake, Arthur Peterson nodded his agreement as he struggled to catch his breath.

Henry Gaithers looked suspiciously at the endorsed traveler's checks. "Arden Crandall? I thought your name was McCauley!"

"Crandall is my maiden name," Arden answered quickly, before anyone else could ask another question. "I can give you identification to prove it."

Gaithers looked doubtful. For a moment it looked as if he might change his mind. "Well, I don't know about that. There are too many con artists running around. What do you think, Cindy?"

"Shame on you, Henry. If Arden says her maiden name was Crandall, that's good enough for me!" his wife answered stoutly.

Luke stepped in front of Arden. "What are you doing here again, Mrs. Peterson?"

"Well, I never!" Arden's aunt replied. "If you must know, Mr. McCauley, as long as her father isn't here to stop her, I've decided it's my duty as Arden's aunt to save her from this foolishness!"

"Wow! Do you mean you two eloped?" Her interest piqued, Cindy asked brightly. "No wonder I felt there was something different between your wedding jitters and mine!"

Eloped! The romantic word sent the brides oohing and aahing.

Luke ground his teeth. Airing his and Arden's personal history in front of strangers, even if it wasn't true, was enough to send him up a wall.

It seemed as if from the moment he'd laid eyes on Arden, it had been one damn thing after another to put him into the limelight. And all of them had revealed his identity. As for his ability to quietly fade into the sunset somewhere south of Cancún, it looked as if that was becoming less and less a viable option.

"Mrs. Peterson," Luke said patiently, although inside he felt as though his nerves were wound tighter than a rubber band, "In spite of what you think, Arden is old enough to know what she wants. She doesn't need saving. And if she did, I'm here to see to it."

"Is this the way you intend to save her?" Jane Peterson asked, pointing dramatically to Arden. "Just take a look at her!"

All eyes swiveled to Arden.

The last of Arden's curls had come loose from their mooring on top of her head and had fallen in uneven lengths to her shoulders. Golden tendrils fell across her forehead. What little makeup she'd had on to start with was off. Her face was pale with fatigue and embarrassment. The I Love NY sweatshirt he'd bought for her was wrinkled and covered with smudges. The white velvet wedding dress that showed underneath was more bedraggled than ever. As for her once-white satin shoes, they'd seen the last of better days.

She'd never looked more beautiful.

And never so endearing.

"She looks fine to me," Luke said as he gathered Arden closer to him. "Look, Mrs. Peterson, Arden has explained everything to her father. Whatever he believes is between the two of them. If you care for your niece, why don't you think about what this is doing to her and just leave her alone?"

"Hiram hasn't seen what his daughter looks like since she ran away! But I fixed that. After I told him what I saw, he's sure to come here to bring her home!"

Arden cringed inside as all eyes swung back to her.

"Wow! This is better than watching the television soaps!" Cindy exclaimed happily. "So, what are you two going to do now that Arden's father knows where she is?"

At the question, Luke felt as if he'd been socked in the solar plexus. What *was* he going to do now?

Arden stirred out of Luke's arms and spoke up. "Aunt Jane, I'm sorry if I disappoint you. But I'm old enough to take responsibility for my own life. I told that to Dad. In time, I'm sure he'll come to understand. I wish you would try to understand, too."

"Humph!" Jane Peterson regarded Arden with distaste. "One thing I do know, young lady—marry in haste, repent at leisure!"

Luke was proud of the way Arden stood up for herself. She might not need him to defend her, but from the weary look about her, she looked as if she'd had enough.

It was more than time to put an end to the impromptu shower.

"We're going to get a few hours shut-eye and wait for the storm to break," Luke remarked. He looked pointedly at Jane Peterson. "Why don't you just leave well enough alone, forget about us and go on your own vacation?"

Arthur Peterson finally stirred himself. "Jane dear, the man's right. If Arden is really his wife, it's none of our business. Come on, let's go."

"*If* Arden is his wife!" Jane Peterson studied Luke carefully. "Not that it makes a difference. I still say the man's a criminal," she announced to the spectators. "Just look at that handcuff he has around his wrist!"

Avid eyes fastened themselves on Luke's left wrist. A few brides gasped. A man chuckled. "Say, I'll bet this is a TV movie being filmed and nobody told us! Where do you suppose the cameras are?" he said, craning his head. "I want to know when it's going to air on TV."

Arden's aunt silenced him with a cold stare. "How do I know this man hasn't kidnapped my niece, or at least brainwashed her so she doesn't have a mind of her own?"

Luke watched the mood of the crowd change. The damage had been done. From the looks of things, some in the crowd believed her. He didn't care about himself, he was used to suspicious looks and questions. But it was different with Arden. Someday she might return home. If nothing else, he had her reputation to consider.

"No sir," Jane Peterson added adamantly, "I'm not going to leave until I know Arden's safe!"

Luke turned his full dark gaze on the angry woman. "Perhaps it would be a good idea for you to leave now before this goes any further."

Arden's aunt gasped at the menacing sound of his voice. Some of the starch seemed to go out of her, but not all. Women like her seldom gave up easily. Luke knew that from experience. Now he not only had Hoyt and his threats to contend with, he had this foolish woman on his and Arden's backs. From her expression, he hadn't heard the last of her.

"Well, perhaps," she conceded. "But I won't be far away. I'm going to keep my eyes on you. Call out if you need me," she told Arden defiantly.

Luke managed not to groan. At the fringe of the crowd surrounding them, he caught a glimpse of a grinning Hoyt. And considering the attention their impromptu bridal shower was attracting, it was only a matter of time before the guy would be joined by a few other unwanted spectators, Airport Security included.

"Come on, Arden." He took her arm. "It's time to go now. I'm sure things will look better to everyone in a couple of hours." He took in the expression on Arden's unhappy face and drooping figure. She looked as if she couldn't stand up any longer, and certainly not under her aunt's accusing eyes. "Let's say goodbye to everyone. And I do mean goodbye," he added as he turned his gaze on Jane Peterson.

One thing he knew for sure: Jane Peterson's eyes weren't the only eyes he knew would be watching them.

THE KEYS Henry Gaithers had handed her seemed to burn the palm of her hand. In her exhausted mind, the gates of perdition her father had threatened her with appeared ready to swing open and swallow her.

The thought of being alone, totally alone, in a secluded roomette with Luke filled Arden with fear, desire and more than a little excitement. Excitement of the kind she'd been taught not to contemplate, except in a biblical sense and only with her husband.

An inner voice was urging caution.

Of course, so far everything had turned out all right. Meeting Luke had made her fantasy of someday finding a heroic and strong man had come true, even if nothing in her original fantasy had included a honeymoon night.

Being stranded with hundreds of strangers in a blinding snowstorm seemed to make the story and the spirit of Christmas come alive. The birth of tiny Noel Alcott had been a miracle. Luke's thoughtful gesture of buying her gifts she might otherwise never have received on this strange Christmas morning had been touching.

The wedding reception and the bridal shower had taken her by surprise, but they'd added excitement to what would otherwise have been a long and dreary night.

Notwithstanding the theft of her luggage, tonight's adventures with Luke had added spice, mystery and a sense of adventure on her road to freedom and independence. Even meeting her aunt and uncle hadn't managed to ruin that for her. Not as long as Luke was with her. But all these adventures had taken place in full view of hundreds of people.

Now, being alone with Luke was a whole different story.

Chapter Eleven

"It doesn't look like much, does it?" Luke remarked when he opened the door to the roomette.

"No, it doesn't." Arden ventured a smile as she glanced around the Spartan quarters. "But I guess it's better than sitting on the floor in the cold for the rest of the night. This is bound to be warmer."

At first glance the room looked to be hardly larger than a walk-in closet. At second glance it wasn't much larger. A pull-down cot was latched to one of the undecorated light green walls. In the far corner, there was a toilet and a minuscule shower enclosed by a transparent curtain. On the wall beside the shower, a lone large towel hung from a rack, a large black-and-white clock above it. A wrapped utilitarian bar of soap was on a soap dish. By the door sat a lone chair.

The only relief the accommodations boasted was a bit of graffiti scrawled above the toilet—Mario slept here. Beneath it someone had added, Me, Too!

When Luke saw the sign, he hid a grin and covertly studied the size of the cot. Whoever Mario had been, he'd obviously been happy. Maybe the cot *was* big enough for two.

He kept his mind off the narrow bed with an effort. "As a matter of fact," he remarked with a casual air, "the accommodations remind me of some aboard a tramp steamer. Of course, I'm sure cruise ships are different. Without the graffiti, of course."

The starkness of the room troubled Luke as he unlatched and lowered the cot. Arden deserved more than an excuse for a bed. And certainly, after all she'd been through tonight, more luxurious accommodations than the small, stark room.

He thought of a South American custom where the marital bed of a newlywed couple was strewn with rose petals to ensure their fragrance would rub off on the lovers' flesh as they joined to become one. And to ensure that their future life together would be as sweet.

He wished he could have managed to arrange a bed of rose petals for Arden.

Of course they weren't really married and this wasn't their wedding night, he reminded himself as he pulled his thoughts back to reality. And, considering his companion, the scenes he was mentally visualizing were unrealistic as hell.

From the quizzical look on her face as she regarded the bed, he realized Arden hadn't changed that much from being a minister's daughter. Dreaming of finding independence and adventure might have been natural for someone raised like her, but tonight's adventures and their possible outcome was obviously a whole new scenario for her.

"Are you really going to stay in here, too?" she asked, turning her questioning blue eyes on him. A frown crinkled her forehead as she glanced at him and back to the cot.

"I was considering it." Luke sensed from the expression on her face the chances of anything intimate was fast becoming slim. Maybe he'd read more into her question than she'd intended.

"Where are you going to sleep?" Arden asked, staring as if mesmerized at the narrow bed. A bed clearly designed for single occupancy.

Luke smothered a groan. She may have told him tonight had been miraculous and fun, but spending the night alone with him in that narrow space was something she obviously hadn't seriously considered.

"I can take the floor," he answered with a rueful smile. "I've kinda gotten used to it."

Arden tore her gaze from the cot, took a good look at Luke and felt herself blush. If he only knew, she'd gotten used to a few things herself—being warmed by his solid, male strength for one.

There was that air of sensuality about him that had dared her to consider something more. There was her longing to be held in his arms again, if only for a little while. To forget parental warnings and to revel in what her senses cried for—the taste of his hard lips on hers, the feel of his solid arms holding her to him, the scent of his maleness. To show him the love she felt growing inside her in spite of the few short hours they'd known each other.

And to forget they would be saying goodbye in the morning.

Margo's off-the-wall notes she'd slipped into Arden's bridal shower gift popped into her mind. It made her aware of the hesitancy in Luke's voice that seemed to suggest he also wanted something more from her before they parted and that he couldn't bring himself to ask.

She fought off the inhibitions that had been conditioned into her and thought of the possibilities at hand. One was becoming obvious. She would have to put aside the strict moral code she'd been taught if there was going to be any hope of making her fantasy of love with this handsome stranger come true. A fantasy that had been born almost in the moment she'd set eyes on Luke's dark and mysterious appearance. And in the moment she'd found the real man beneath the surface.

The hard veneer he'd displayed turned soft when he was alone with her. His values, when he'd spoken of Christmas mornings and gifts under the tree, appeared to be not much different from hers, no matter what he'd said. And not when he'd given her the Christmas gifts she might otherwise never have had.

Whatever else he may be, it was obvious Luke was a gentleman. And now that he'd heard her father's wrath, he was obviously trying to be more circumspect than ever.

If she was going to experience THE GREAT AWAKENING, she would have to make the first move.

With or without Margo's well-meaning hints.

If tonight was going to be the last one she and Luke would spend together, she yearned to know him in the biblical sense she'd been warned against. She knew, though, that if she gave in to her desire for Luke, the reality was that by morning she'd find herself alone.

From the luminous expression in her eyes, Luke sensed that part of what Arden was thinking mirrored his own growing desire. If she were anyone else, he could have probably talked her into something more than a goodbye embrace. But this was Arden. And it was her innocent naïveté that deterred him.

He thought of his past relationships. Always temporary, never lasting. Not that he'd ever pretended otherwise. He might not always have behaved as a saint, but he liked to think he'd always been a decent man.

He noticed fragments of mistletoe that had been tossed in the air in the terminal and were scattered in Arden's hair, a clear invitation to a kiss. And much more, if she'd only realized how tempting she was. Nothing in her background seemed to suggest she was aware of her latent sensuality.

He contented himself with gently picking the mistletoe leaves from her hair. He was taken by surprise when her hand unexpectedly reached to cover his. He could feel the growing air of expectancy crackle through the room.

He fought the tug on his heartstrings as he gazed down at Arden. Their mutual attraction aside, he was going to be in big trouble if the surprising, tender awareness he felt for her didn't quit, or if it turned into something more serious.

"Tell you what," he said into her silence. "I'll just go on outside for a few minutes until you've showered and changed."

"Yes, of course, maybe it would be better," she

answered. Her blush as she turned away was enough to light up the room.

He liked the way she walked, unconsciously swinging her hips. He liked the way the bright overhead lights highlighted the golden glint in her hair. In fact, he liked everything about Arden.

Visions of holding her in his arms in the borrowed bridal negligee grew stronger as he gazed after her. He stirred restlessly as his body reacted to the thought.

"Call out when you're ready," he replied, pulling his overcoat more closely around him to hide his physical reaction. "I'll be right outside the door."

He breathed a sigh of relief when the door to the roomette closed behind him. A fragment of a sermon he'd once heard in an American evangelist church down South America way came to mind. "Get thee behind me, Satan!"

As far as he was concerned, taking Arden in his arms and making love to her would have the more likely result of visiting Heaven than Hades. He cursed softly. At the rate he was going, it looked as if he was never likely to find out.

"Gotcha!"

Luke snapped out of his sensuous reverie. With his hands in his coat pockets to simulate guns, Hoyt stood there grinning at him.

"Hey, don't worry," the beady-eyed man said slyly when he'd gotten Luke's attention. He took out his hands and turned them palms up to Luke to show there was nothing in them. "I was only kidding. This ain't the time I was talking about. I just wanted you to know I haven't forgotten you."

"And I haven't forgotten you, either," Luke spat out between cold, hard lips. Damn the man! The warm mood of the moment before vanished as if it had been snuffed out by the snowstorm outside the terminal. "You can bet your life on it. And if you keep this up, you *will* be betting your life!"

"Got your girl inside, I hear."

Hoyt's raised eyebrows and suggestive smile fed Luke's fury. Only the time and the place and the need to protect Arden kept him from smashing a fist into that shifty smile on the guy's face. "That's none of your business!" he answered, clenching his fists.

"Hey, back off, I was just joking." Hoyt threw up his hands again and broke into a broad, satisfied grin. "But I wouldn't mind having a sample of what the lady has to offer. Must be really something to interest a guy like you."

"I'll give you ten seconds to get out of my sight," Luke answered, levering himself away from the door behind him. "If I catch you hanging around here again, I won't wait for a better time and place. And when I get through with you, there won't be enough left of you for a hearing to keep you out of prison."

"Not with that briefcase you have chained to your wrist, you won't," Hoyt said defiantly. "What's in there, anyway?"

"Nothing that would interest you," Luke replied. "Why don't you crawl back into your hole until your supplier arrives?"

"Who told you I was waiting for my supplier?" Hoyt's grin abruptly disappeared. His eyes narrowed, his face hardened into a dark scowl. "You're going to have to prove it!"

"You just proved it," Luke answered. "If I wasn't sure of it before, I'm sure of it now." He took a menacing step closer to Hoyt. "Now get lost while you still have two unbroken legs."

"Oh, yeah?" Hoyt sputtered. "But you'd better watch your back. And your lady friend's, too."

Luke drew a deep breath to control his anger as Hoyt swaggered away. Taking care of Arden's safety was already number one on his priority list. He swore to be more watchful than ever.

"Luke!" He heard Arden call through the door.

He shook off the feeling of dread that came over him at the sound of her voice. Hoyt had been right. There wasn't much he could do to protect Arden with the damn briefcase getting in the way.

For Arden's sake, maybe he'd have to reorganize his priorities.

He opened the door to the roomette expecting to find Arden snugly in bed. Instead, he found her waiting for him gowned in an outrageous confection of silk and lace designed to drive a man out of his mind. The music box tinkled in the background, Santa rode his sleigh across its red lacquer cover. The sensuous fragrance of soap and perfume filled the air.

Satan had surfaced to tempt him in all his glory. Suddenly Luke wasn't sure he had the strength to put temptation behind him. Not with the inviting smile on Arden's face. Did she realize what she was doing to him?

"I figured you'd be in bed by now, g-getting some

rest," he stammered, closing the door behind him. On second thought, he turned back and checked the locks. After his latest run-in with Hoyt, he would have thought a sexual encounter would have been the farthest thing from his mind. But it wasn't. Gazing at the willowy Arden, he suddenly became willing to gamble with the devil.

She was a mixture of mischievous young girl and seductive woman. A combination of innocence and naïveté, of innate courage and of feminine independence all at the same time. The antithesis of any woman he'd ever met in his travels around the world.

Fortunately for Arden's sake, he thought dimly as he fought to control his raging testosterone, she didn't know what she was doing to him. Surely, her background must have sheltered her from the more sophisticated times she was living in. And from knowing men like himself.

She needed a husband who understood the woman who had blossomed in front of his eyes tonight, he told himself before he let himself get carried away. A man who loved her enough to allow her the freedom to continue to grow, to appreciate the wonderful bundle of womanhood that was Arden.

She deserved the best to introduce her to what the evangelist had called carnal knowledge. Honesty reminded him he wasn't it.

Arden gazed back at Luke with a heightened sense of awareness. She could tell that whatever his experiences with women had been in the past, he was wary of her. Even after she thought she'd issued a clear invitation.

It was time to put the first of Margo's tutelage into practice: "Get him to talk about himself. Men love it when they think you're a good listener. And while he's talking, start the touching."

Touching?

Talking Arden understood, she'd listened to John talk about himself long enough. But touching? With Luke dressed in a suit, tie and overcoat? Just where was she to touch?

"There's time enough to rest later," she said as she slowly walked toward him. "I thought we could talk a little first."

"Talk? Now?" He swallowed hard as he stared at Arden's swinging hips. They were even more enticing in a sheer negligee than they'd been under her sweatshirt. "We've done nothing but talk all night."

"Yes, but not enough," she answered. "Maybe that's the trouble. All you've ever told me is why I should forget I ever met you. But if I'm never going to see you again, the least you could do is to tell me a little more about you."

"For heaven's sakes, why?"

"To give me something to remember you by," she replied softly.

Luke backed away. A few more inches and they would be toe to toe, head to head and chest to chest. Her perfumed scent wafted through the air, her rosy flesh shone through pristine lace to add to the temptation.

He swallowed the lump that rose in his throat and hurriedly put the briefcase between them. She might be unsophisticated and, he suspected, a novice to seduction. But pretty soon she was sure to realize how much he was aware of her.

"It's getting kind of hot in here, isn't it?" he asked as he loosened his tie and drew his hand across his forehead with his free hand.

"Really? I hadn't noticed," Arden replied, her gaze fixed firmly on his chest. "Why don't you unbutton your suit jacket?"

Unbutton his jacket? Luke blinked. Definitely not! It would be taking off the armor he'd intentionally surrounded himself with through the years to keep from feeling too much, caring too much.

"And maybe your shirt?"

"Thanks, no. I'm not that warm," he answered warily as he noted the growing interest in Arden's eyes.

"Then tell me a little about yourself," she asked. "What were you like when you were growing up?"

Grateful at the new direction in which things were going, Luke breathed a sigh of relief. Temptation was sure as hell easier to avoid as long as he was fully dressed. He was willing to talk about anything as long as it wasn't the subject of unbuttoning his clothing.

"I was raised in a small town in the mid-west," he began, forcing his thoughts off Arden and the fixed way she was studying his chest. "My dad had a drugstore and expected me to take it over someday. I had other ideas."

"You didn't want to become a pharmacist?"

"No. I guess I was much the same then as I am now," he answered, deliberately fighting the desire to satisfy the need in her eyes. And to hide the one coursing through him.

He tried to concentrate on the daredevil young boy he'd been, not so different from the man he'd become. Confessing he might be less than a knight in shining armor didn't come easily. But there was that something about Arden that made him want to tell the truth.

"I was sure there were exciting adventures waiting for me around every corner. You might say I made sure I found them or that they found me. Unfortunately, I can't say I was proud of them all."

"Is that how you got the scar?" Her fingers slid gently across the scar on his chin and lingered on his lips. It felt to him as if her fingers were sliding up and down his spine.

"I'm afraid so." He had a whole lot more scars on his body and in his mind that he was just as glad she couldn't see.

"We are a lot alike, then, aren't we?" Arden said, gazing into his troubled dark eyes. "All my life I've wanted independence and more excitement and freedom than I had under my father's care. But it wasn't easy to break away. Until now."

"I guess it's different with girls," Luke answered. Not that he was sure he was making sense after the way his thoughts kept focusing on the pink flesh peeking out from under Arden's negligee. "At least my sister used to say so. She stayed home and married the boy next door. They run the drugstore now."

He took a step backward. Another few inches and he'd be backed against the door.

"Yes," Arden answered absently as she followed

him. "I couldn't bring myself to break loose. That is, until the time came for me to marry John." She moved closer and reached for his tie. "Here, let me help you with that."

Luke swallowed hard. He was a red-blooded man responding to a sexy woman. The feathery touch of her fingers brushing against his chin wasn't doing a damn thing to cool off that blood.

"Say, it's almost three-thirty in the morning," he said, grabbing her hand before she went too far. He *had* to keep his clothes on if he was going to see this night through. "If you're going to get any rest, you'd better hop into bed. I'm beat, too. I'll just make myself comfortable here on the floor."

Arden blinked. Margo's instructions didn't seem to be working. But then, maybe Margo's idea of losing one's virginity wasn't going to work with Luke. She was on her own.

"Are you sure that's what you want to do?"

"You bet." The flustered look he gave her suggested that what he wanted to do and what he was going to do were two different stories.

A part of Luke told him to open the door and run. The other part of him wanted to throw his conscience to the winds and pull Arden into his arms. To caress the bare skin under the sheer robe, to inhale her fragrance, to savor every moment of the woman he'd come to care for.

Care for?

The shock of putting words to what his mind and his body were telling him hit him hard. Especially when he realized the truth was that he more than cared for Arden. And cared in a way that hungered for more of her than her body for the next few hours. To his surprise, he wanted to spend a lifetime with her in his arms.

"Now what are you going to do?" Arden asked, hesitating beside the bed. She'd been as up-front as she'd dared to be. Maybe she'd gone about it the wrong way.

"Move on to the next job," he answered, his eyes averted. "Now, why don't you call it a night?"

Arden gave in and slid under the covers. More to take the time to mentally review what was next on Margo's list than to rest.

"You might want to turn your back," she heard Luke remark. "I'm going to try to make myself comfortable."

Next item on Margo's list: "Get him to touch you. You'll know the right places."

Even Margo hadn't dared to go into details, but Arden had a pretty good idea where those places were, judging from the way her body had responded to him.

Visions of bare bodies straining flesh to flesh rose before her eyes. She pictured wrapping herself around a hard, warm male body under a hot tropical sun. Of strong arms holding her, hard lips tasting hers. Of a hand touching her in places she could only dare to imagine.

And of a love nest burrowed in hot, white tropical sands. Of clear, blue waters that would cool her heated flesh.

When she finally dared to turn around, it was to find Luke stretched out on the floor. Although his left arm was still tangled in his overcoat, he'd managed to take it off his right shoulder and put it and the briefcase behind his head. He'd taken off his shoes. His coat jacket and the top few buttons of his shirt were unbuttoned.

"Are you sure you don't want to join me?" she asked leaning over the edge of the cot, inches away from his dark eyes.

Luke smothered a groan. A habit of his lately, she noted with a smile of satisfaction. So he wasn't immune to her, after all.

"Arden, if I do," he said tightly, "I'm afraid there might be some consequences you might not want."

"Consequences?"

"Come on," Luke said bluntly, "surely you must have heard something about a man's physical reaction when he gets that close to a woman as intriguing as you."

Intriguing? No one had ever suggested she was intriguing before. Even John had never said anything as suggestive or complimentary. Not even in his more amorous moments.

"No, not much." She carefully schooled her voice to hide the qualms she felt at what she was about to suggest. "But I'd like to learn more."

Luke sensed how difficult it was for Arden to be so frank and honest with him. And he knew what might happen if he blew the moment. He'd been avoiding relationships for years, but tonight was different. Arden was different. He'd never known anyone like her. He closed his eyes, willing himself to remember the next few hours were critical.

"Arden, I'll try be honest with you," he managed to say as he smothered a groan of frustration. "I care for you, but not enough for a lifetime. I don't think I'm the man to teach you the man/woman thing."

"Well, I do," she answered softly. "You, and only you. And only because I care for you very much. In a way I've never cared for any man before."

The look in her eyes undid him.

Muttering a prayer, that he would be able to handle the situation without frightening Arden or scaring her off, he rose to sit at the edge of the bed. He vowed to himself he would be the tender lover she was entitled to. "You're sure?"

"I'm sure."

Luke sensed Arden was ready to become a woman in every sense of the word. Some other man might use her and leave her emotionally bruised. Some other man might not realize the treasure that Arden was, but he did. He couldn't face the idea of Arden with any other man but him.

He ignored the inner voice that urged him to run before he did something he might live to regret. But gazing down at Arden, he knew it was too late.

He gave in to the desire that blazed inside him. He bent and gently ran his tongue over the lips that seemed to taste of honey. Inhaled the scent of the lily of the valley shampoo a thoughtful bride had given Arden for her wedding night. When her arms rose to encircle his head, he lost himself in the magic that was Arden.

She undid the first few buttons on his shirt and slid her fingers across his chest, at first hesitantly, then more urgently. His muscles tensed when she bent to listen to the steady rhythm of his heart.

He opened the rest of the buttons on his shirt to give her entry and watched the wonder that filled her eyes. The touch of her fingertips gliding across his skin sent waves of pleasure coursing through him.

"My turn," he said softly as he reached for the ribbons that closed the sheer negligee at her neck. It was difficult with the suitcase and the overcoat dragging at his side. He muttered a soft curse under his breath as he overcame the obstacle. He slid the robe off her shoulders, let his fingers drift over her bare shoulder to the hollow between her breasts.

"You're so beautiful," he said softly as he lowered his lips to the breasts she offered him. "Beautiful, inside and out." He teased her taut breasts with his tongue.

"You're sure you want this? I can stop now." He laughed shakily. "But I warn you I can't guarantee I'll be able to stop later."

She shook her head. "Don't stop," she whispered. Desire drove Margo's list out of Arden's mind. She opened her arms and folded him to her. Her dreams were coming true. Maybe not exactly in the approved way she'd been taught, but Luke was the man she wanted to take her to THE GREAT AWAKENING. Tomorrow would have to take care of itself.

"Here, wait a minute," he told her. "It's going to be a little awkward, but if you're willing to chance a few more black-and-blue marks, I think we can manage."

He paused to fumble in his wallet. He wasn't going

to do anything that might endanger Arden, now or in the future.

This was what she had been waiting for. To be this man's woman, if only for tonight. And to make him hers, if only for tonight.

He was fast becoming more than just a fantasy. He was the personified dream of a man she could love. He was vibrant, caring, a man of mystery, a man with an edge that drove him to live his dreams as no ordinary man could. But then, he was no ordinary man.

Luke gently urged her to remove her robe and her nightgown. He wouldn't let her be shy. "I want to see all of you," he told her. Soon his passion became her own.

"When you think of this, remember that I care for you," he murmured.

"And that I care for you," she sighed into his lips. "I want to feel you all over, too."

"Sorry, my sweet, that's impossible. But I'll do the best I can." He pulled his suit jacket and shirt as far away from his body as he could without taking them off. "I'm afraid the rest will have to wait until another time," he said ruefully.

Would there be another night like tonight? Arden wondered dimly as Luke took her to him. Would there be another chance to know all of the man in her arms?

She instinctively stiffened when Luke gently prodded her legs apart and murmured soothing words. Now that the moment had come that would change her forever, doubt flickered in the back of her mind. Was she right in giving herself to her fantasy? Was that all Luke was? A fantasy?

From the urgent way he held her to him, she knew there was no turning back. Not now. The fantasy man had disappeared in the sensuous haze of reality. Luke was a flesh-and-blood man and, for the moment, hers. The man she cared for, and the man who cared for her.

The man she'd chosen herself, instead of one her father had chosen for her.

With a sigh she lost herself in his arms.

Chapter Twelve

The sound of water running in the shower awakened Arden. It took a few moments for her to remember where she was and whom she'd been with. Luke...she smiled as she lay back against the pillow to relive the way he'd made love to her: so soft, so tender and caring. Her body, bruised with his kisses, ached pleasurably. Her skin still tingled where his unshaven cheeks had brushed against her skin.

Even the briefcase had been forgotten while he'd stirred her senses, made her feel womanly, alive.

A thousand nerve endings throbbed as her thoughts swirled around her. Warm memories held her captive.

If this had been THE AWAKENING Margo had hinted about, it had been worth waiting until Luke had come along. Not that she'd needed Margo's notes after the first few moments in his arms. Loving him had come to her naturally.

A quick glance showed her his trousers were still lying on the edge of the cot. She smiled as she visualized him trying to take a shower dodging the water with the remainder of his clothing bundled around his arm.

The thought of his bronzed body brought her wide awake. A blush cascaded over her. She wanted to touch him, feel his hard muscular strength straining against her again. She turned to welcome him, ready to tease him into coming back to her. Her smile faded as she caught sight of Luke as he emerged from the shower.

Luke was naked?

Impossible!

But true.

His clothing, including his overcoat, was neatly folded in a pile on the roomette's sole chair. The briefcase that had become so much a part of him was hidden underneath. Only a glimpse of brown leather revealed its presence.

The briefcase was on the chair?

"What do you think you're doing!" she asked as cold reality set in and her sensuous memories vanished. She grabbed her negligee and scrambled out of bed.

Luke froze in the act of reaching for the towel. "Taking a shower," he offered cautiously. He whipped the towel around his lean hips and stood there poised waiting for her next reaction.

She clutched the borrowed white lace gown to her chest. "I can see that! I'm talking about what you look like!"

He glanced down at his body, bare except for the towel. He shrugged as he met her gaze.

This had to be a dream! The last time she'd seen him, the briefcase had been attached to his wrist by the handcuffs and chain that had prevented him from taking off his overcoat, shirt and jacket. He'd worn them the entire time he'd gently initiated her into the ways of a man and a woman.

Now he'd somehow removed his clothing and the briefcase! But how, when he'd assured her he didn't have the key? Hadn't he told her more than once the handcuff couldn't be removed until he delivered the briefcase to the owners of the Majestic Hotel?

If he'd lied about the briefcase, had he lied about caring for her as well?

Head cocked to one side, he continued to eye her warily. If he had any ready answers, it was obvious he wasn't willing to share them with her.

She became more bewildered by each passing moment. How could he act as if there was nothing unusual about his appearance?

"I want to know why you're taking a shower with your clothes off!" she persisted. "*All* of them!"

"The usual reasons," he said lightly. "To shower without getting my clothes wet."

"That's not what I meant, and you know it. You're just stalling for time!" she retorted. "I want to know how you were able to take the handcuff off your wrist now, when you couldn't do it before."

He ran his hand across a damp forelock that persisted in falling over his eye, hesitated before he answered. "I'm sorry, Arden. You were sleeping so soundly, I didn't have the heart to awaken you. I thought I had enough time to shower and be dressed again before you did. Although, maybe I should have told you sooner."

"If you were an honest man, you would have," she

answered, still in a state of shock. "From the way it's beginning to look, I'm not sure what else you may be hiding from me."

"Come on, Arden. Don't be so hard on me. I had my reasons for keeping quiet."

"Reasons! You never intended to tell me the whole truth of who you are or what you're up to, did you?" she demanded, fighting to hold back tears. "What I want to know is how you managed to open the lock on the handcuffs?"

"It's a long story and has nothing to do with you. Or with this," he said gesturing to the narrow cot. He wiped lingering drops of water from his forehead as he reached around her to pick up his trousers. "But believe me when I tell you I never meant to hurt you, or for you to see me like this."

Arden's heart sank as she stared at the man whose powerful body had enthralled her just moments ago. Now its sheer masculine power seemed intimidating.

He shook his head and closed the few steps between them. His jaw clenched as he tried to speak. His sable eyes were shadowed. With concern? Guilt? Remorse? An intense sorrow gripped her as she realized she'd been manipulated by this man as easily as if she'd been a puppet on a string.

How could she have been so wrong about him? How could she have been so naive as to think there was a decent man behind the dark and mysterious edge that had initially attracted her, and heaven help her, attracted her still? Even after he'd told her he wasn't the man she thought he was. And even after he'd warned her he wasn't the man for her?

How could she have given herself to him after she'd been warned repeatedly about the dangers of being attracted to men like him?

She closed her eyes and saw herself as if in a mirror. It was time to take a look at herself, to be honest with herself. Luke had warned her, but she'd still made a conscious decision to give herself to him, anyway. And, to her shame, she'd been the one to force the romance of the moment.

She was no more honest than he was, unless she admitted the truth. She had no right to put the blame on him.

He took another tentative step toward her. He reached for her, dropped his hands when she drew back. "I never meant for this to happen."

"I know you didn't," she agreed. She backed away, feeling as if her heart was breaking. "You only took what I offered. Under the circumstances, I have no right to blame you. But I think I do have the right to question you about the handcuffs."

As their eyes locked, Arden felt the last of her dreams crumble around her feet as surely as the walls of Jericho had fallen after the assault of its defenses by Joshua. But Luke wasn't a Joshua and this wasn't a biblical story. This was real life, and so was Luke.

And somehow she found she wasn't sorry at having given herself to him.

He wasn't only the man she'd conjured up out of her imagination. He was the man who'd introduced her to a side of life she'd longed for. A longing that had begun when she'd met him last night and that had crystallized this morning. A longing that had made her invite him to make love to her.

He was also the man who'd betrayed her trust.

She shook her head, hoping she'd awaken to find this was a dream, after all. That Luke was really the man she'd created in her fantasy instead of the devious man he'd turned out to be.

"You've been living a lie and taking me with you," she said sadly. "Maybe this was all a game and I was just too naive to see it. But if it was only a game, and if you cared for me at all, you should have stopped before it was too late."

"No, Arden, it wasn't a game," Luke said gently, aching to hold her to him, to soothe her hurt, to show her with his love how much he *did* care for her. To show her how deeply he shared her pain. But he didn't dare. Not now, and not until he could manage to restore her trust. And especially not until he could convince her there *was* a decent man waiting for her, even if it wasn't going to be him.

"I couldn't stop myself. Not after I saw you waiting for me with that sweet invitation in your eyes," he answered carefully. "I'd already come to care for you too much to ignore that invitation. I may have been selfish, but if any man was going to teach you the ways of a man with a woman, I wanted it to be me."

Arden gestured as if to push his words away; a tear slid down her cheeks. Icicles formed around his heart at the bleak look in her eyes.

Luke felt devastated, helpless. Her innocent appeal had drawn him almost from the first moment their eyes had met. He damned himself for thinking only of himself and not dreaming of the possible consequences. How could he have been so stupid as to draw her into a tangled web of his own making?

"I couldn't tell you the truth because I couldn't give myself away," he went on. "I didn't dare. I felt I had to behave like the man I outwardly appeared to be— a harmless courier making a delivery. For your sake as well as my own. Believe me when I tell you I had no ulterior motives when I spoke to you the first time." He shook his head. "I can't even explain the instant attraction I felt for you as soon as our eyes met. All I can do is ask you to trust me."

"You didn't have to string me along with the story about the briefcase. Or take advantage of my foolish dreams," she answered sadly. "You let me think you cared. You even let me fall in love with you."

"Ah, Arden," Luke said sadly, aching to take her in his arms and soothe her hurt away. "I don't think you love me. No one could possibly fall in love in one crazy night at an airport."

"I did," she answered quietly, "or I wouldn't have asked you to make love to me. I was never more certain of anything in my life."

"I don't think you know what love is," he said, hoping the regret he felt inside was in his eyes and his voice as he closed the few steps between them. How else would he be able to persuade her he'd meant her no harm?

"I swear I never meant for you to fall in love with me. Or that I even considered letting myself fall in love with you. But you were hard to resist. Actually," he added, glancing at the door behind her, "in this business my life depends on secrecy, on being a loner. The truth is, it's long past the time when I could choose anything else.''

Now he wondered how he'd sunk so low as to contemplate becoming the same kind of man he'd spent twelve long years bringing to justice. Gazing at Arden, he couldn't believe he was even thinking of becoming one of the men he'd hunted.

"But you still took me up on my offer. Knowing all the time you intended to walk away?"

"Even then," he answered. "I'm sorry. Even then." Luke grasped her hands in his, lifted them to his lips and kissed her cold fingers. "Especially then. I couldn't help myself."

She had no idea of the life he'd led before now, Luke mused as he kissed her cold fingers one by one. Of the enemies he'd made, hunting down the wanted criminals the government had hired him to find. Of the inner battle facing him now.

Or that his past might be waiting for him outside the door, maybe even hiding around every corner, every street. And that if he took the contents of the briefcase and disappeared as he'd planned, he would be looking over his shoulder the rest of his life.

As for Arden, he was grateful she had no idea of that past. Nor how important it was now for him to disappear before he took her into danger with him.

Maybe he shouldn't have taken advantage of her naive faith and trust in him. But she'd been too hard to resist. He'd had to make her his, to share her honeyed sweetness if only for tonight.

And, for better or worse, before he disappeared to

put his plans to make a new life for himself into action.

"What kind of man are you?" Arden whispered through her tears. Then she seemed to find the inner strength that demanded answers. "Tell me who you really are! You owe me that much!"

Luke's heart sank. He knew the man he'd been, but what kind of man *had* he become?

Maybe he'd lived in a dark world so long he'd already become no better than the men and women he'd helped to bring to justice. He couldn't tell her that. He couldn't destroy *all* her dreams and her faith in herself.

"To tell the truth, I'm just an ordinary man," he answered. He couldn't tell the whole truth. It was sure to make her hate herself for giving herself to him and hate him for taking what she'd offered. He cradled her cold hands against his chest. "A guy who's surprised to find out how much he cares for you. And," he added with growing wonderment of his own as he gazed into her troubled blue eyes, "it looks as if I might have managed to grow to care for you more than ever in the process."

"Care for me?" She pulled her hands away. "If you cared for me, how could you have taken advantage of my foolish dreams? Especially when it must have been clear to you, you were a man I'd conjured up in my imagination?"

"I couldn't. But honestly, soon after we met last night, it wasn't all pretending," he answered. "I discovered I enjoyed being with you, listening to your dreams, seeing miracles through your eyes. I think I loved you from the time I first laid eyes on you until

I had you warm and willing in my arms." He held her away from him, smiled down into her eyes. "I can't believe I was lucky enough to find someone special like you in a crowded airport of all places. And all in a single night!"

Softly, he stroked her cheek with a forefinger. Smiled to see her blush. "Maybe because it was the spirit of Christmas that mellowed me, but I couldn't help myself when I asked you to join me. And then, I got a kick out of the way you defended me to Airport Security and talked your way out of trouble, mine *and* yours. And the way you found something good in everything and everyone, including a guy like me."

He held his finger across her lips and shook his head as she started to speak. "No, let me finish," he said into her eyes. "I was intrigued by the way you saw a miracle in a baby being born on the floor of an airport terminal. And who could resist a woman who finds such delight in a simple little music box, in a toy Santa and his reindeer and in Christmas mornings."

She leaning helplessly into his chest. "That doesn't explain the briefcase. That doesn't tell me where we go from here."

"I wish I knew," he said softly into her sweet-smelling hair. "I guess I sensed you needed someone to hold you tonight. I wanted that someone to be me. As to where we go from here, I guess I only meant to give us something to remember."

"For only tonight?" He heard the break in her voice.

The question disturbed him. But he owed her the truth. "I've never promised anything else. I couldn't then," he said regretfully, remembering the danger to her if she knew too much of the truth. "I still can't."

The doorknob rattled once, twice, a third time before she could answer. Instinctively she gasped and stiffened in his arms.

He put his finger to her lips and shook his head. "If it's the man I think it is," he whispered, "I want him to believe we've vacated the roomette. For both our sakes. Okay?"

No matter how he wanted to rid himself of Hoyt once and for all, he had to hide behind the door to the roomette like a coward. For Arden's sake. He had no weapons to fight back with, only his silence.

He needed time. He needed time to make Arden believe in him and in herself before they said goodbye. He couldn't leave her like this, uncertain of herself and her decision to find the independence to be her own woman. Not when an unknown future stretched before her. And not when his ill-advised passion might disillusion her about men and send her back into the safety of her fiancé's arms.

The doorknob rattled again. Arden returned his warning gaze. He set her aside, ready in case the would-be intruder made his way inside the roomette. Although the door held, he knew from experience there were ways to open it if someone had a passkey— or worse.

"So, what do you say, Arden?" he asked in as casual a voice as he could muster when the footsteps outside the door finally faded away. He had to end this now, send her on her way. If anyone's heart was going to be broken, it was going to have to be his. "Now that you know I never meant to hurt you, can we at least part as friends?''

He wanted to be more than friends, but he couldn't tell her so. Not after she'd told him she was falling in love with him. Friends were safer than lovers.

''Is that what this has been about—friendship?''

''Partly,'' he answered softly, brushing her cheek with fingers that ached to do more. ''I've shown you the rest.''

Arden regarded him steadily. How could she have thrown aside all she'd ever known, all she'd ever been taught, to take up with a man whose values were so different from hers? How could she be friends with this man to whom she'd so foolishly given herself? Given herself for the first time, and *only* because it had been him?

In the course of the hours since they'd met, had she been guilty of creating a fantasy man, who actually had feet of clay and lies in his heart?

Hadn't he known how meaningful their coming together would be for her? How could she be friends when her heart said yes and her head said no? She'd always believed the mind controls the body, but she was wrong. It was the heart. She still wanted him.

''Arden?''

She looked up into his questioning eyes, still trying to search for answers.

''I asked if we could at least be friends?''

Arden shook her head. ''No,'' she answered slowly. ''Not just friends. Not after this. And not until I have a chance to think, to find out who I really am. If the independence I thought I wanted was real.''

Luke's blood turned cold. What had he done to this special woman to rob her of the confidence that had brought her so trustfully into his arms? "Find yourself?"

"Yes," she answered sadly as she drew away from him. "I don't know who I am anymore. A woman or a spoiled and willful girl just like Aunt Jane said I am. I don't even know if I can trust my own judgment anymore," she added. "The first thing I was taught as a child was to know right from wrong. Now I don't even know if I'm able to do that anymore."

"Arden, please, don't put yourself through this!" Luke pleaded, as he saw the grief in her exquisite eyes. "You're more of a real human being than most I've met. If anyone is to blame for what happened tonight, it's me. I've been around the block, I should have known better. You're everything that's right in this crazy world of ours!" He tried to hold her, but she shook her head and pulled away.

"If I could only believe that, but I don't think I can," she said, turning back to the cot. "I have to find my clothes, dress and leave."

"Leave? For where?"

"Someplace alone where I can think. At least until I can trust myself and my judgment," she answered with a catch in her voice.

"Does that mean you intend to go back and marry this fiancé of yours?"

"No. John's not my fiancé anymore. Anyway, after yesterday, he won't want me. He deserves someone better."

Luke became angry, angry at himself for what he'd done to Arden to destroy her faith in herself.

"There *isn't* anyone better than you! A guy would have to be crazy not to realize it!" He took her in his arms, crushed her to him. He couldn't let her go like this. He had to restore her confidence in herself. Show her what a wonderful and worthy woman she was. Show her how much he cared for her, that their sensual encounter meant more to him than a one-night stand. He had to do this, no matter what, no matter how long it might take. His own plans would have to take second place for now.

It had taken him a lifetime to find someone like Arden, who restored his own faith in the world around him. And in himself.

Was what he'd been planning worth losing Arden?

"You're not going back!" he said vigorously. "At least, not back to your father's house. No," he added firmly as she started to protest, "we're not going anywhere until we come to an understanding. I care for you too much to let you go doubting yourself. If we can't settle this now, we'll go on to Cancún and talk this out. But you're not going home."

She met his eyes, tears still shadowing her clear blue eyes. "I thought you only wanted to be friends?"

"Come here and I'll show you how I feel about you," Luke answered, drawing her back into his arms. He had to take the hurt from her eyes. The idea of remaining only friends with her evaporated in a moment of truth. He loved this woman.

"Sweetheart, sometimes words aren't enough," he told her. "Sometimes words can't say it all. Come

back here and let me show you how much you've
come to mean to me."

"In spite of everything you said about the dangers
facing you that keep us apart?"

"In spite of everything," he agreed as he drew the
negligee out of her cold hands. "The first time we met,
I offered to warm you with my coat, remember? I
didn't know it then, but it turned out to be the best
idea I'd ever come up with.

"And this time," he added softly into her lumines-
cent eyes, "I intend to warm you in another way."

He lowered Arden to the cot, dropped the towel
from around his hips and joined her.

"The first time was for you. This time it will be for
both of us. No," he said moving away the hands she
held against her chest to cover herself. "I want to see
every adorable inch of you, to love every inch of
you."

Under his impassioned gaze, Arden shut out her
doubts and put her arms around him. Everything about
her life had been planned for her until now. This man
was her choice. A heated sensation spread through her
as she realized this time his loving was going to be a
new experience from the one last night. The first time,
he'd taken care to arouse her, to make her want him,
to make her welcome him. He'd taken her with a tenderness she would remember forever. But even as he'd
given her pleasure, she'd somehow sensed he'd been
holding something back, fearful of offending or frightening her. Now she would know the full meaning of
making love.

He loved her first with his lips, nibbling gently on

hers until she opened to him. With soft whispers of reassurance, he slid his lips over her neck, her shoulders, breasts and down to her hips, lingering only long enough until she stirred with passion. When he moved back to her lips, she returned his kiss with all the desire that welled up in her. Her body burned with wanting; the need for him, built up inside of her and threatened to burst.

He loved her with his hands, tenderly brushing the sensitive skin between her breasts, the tips of her breasts, the curve of her waist and inner thighs. With soft whispers of pleasure, he placed kisses where his hands had traveled, until she was on fire.

Instinctively she reached for him to end the wanting, only to hear him whisper, "Soon."

He loved her with his glistening body, covering her until she felt mindless with the need to become part of him.

When he finally joined their bodies, Arden's faith in herself was reborn. This was the man she'd chosen for her lover, this was the man she would remember forever...even if this was to be the last night they spent together. The questions about the briefcase and his past vanished in a haze of pleasure.

She returned his passion and his ardor with every ounce of love in her, until the stars that seemed to have gathered behind her eyes broke in a brilliant shower to cover them with their light.

Luke loved her. In her world, he couldn't possibly make such wondrous love to her without meaning every fiery touch, every lingering kiss.

"When did you fall in love with me?" she asked,

when Luke finally fell to his side, pulled her to his chest and looked down at her with that quirky smile that had attracted her from the first moment their eyes had met.

He kissed her on the tip of her nose. "Just like a woman, wanting to talk at a time like this," he answered with a light laugh.

"I need to know."

Unaccustomed to speaking openly of love, Luke found it hard to voice his thoughts. But he could see she needed reassurance. "Actually, that's an easy question to answer," he said solemnly when she prodded his shoulder. "It was twice. The first time was when you stood up to a security guard two times your size, defending me as if I actually *was* your husband. Then, I was sure of it when I saw how happy you were when I gave you that funny little music box."

He untangled himself long enough to reach for the music box and to set the sleigh in motion. Smiling, he returned Santa's wave as the little figure passed.

"So, what's good for the goose is good for the gander," he joked as he took her comfortably back into his arms. He felt a little foolish, but all things considered, he'd done more than a few foolish things tonight. "When did you fall in love with me?"

"Only once, but it seems as if I've loved you forever," Arden answered. She cradled his head and drew him down for a lingering kiss. "When you held little Noel in your hands and smiled down at him so tenderly before you handed him to his mother."

Luke rewarded her with another kiss. In moments, they returned to a special world of their own, while the little red music box went round and round on its red lacquer surface until it wound down.

"So, tell me," Luke asked later. "Now do you believe I care for you? That I never intended to hurt you?" he teased tenderly, running a questing forefinger across her lips.

"Yes, I do," she whispered into his sable eyes, warmed with love, compassion and understanding. He couldn't have made such tender, passionate love to her if he hadn't really cared for her. This *was* the man she'd dreamed about long before she'd met and fallen in love with him. He *was* a flesh-and-blood man, not just a fantasy. She ran a searching finger across the scar under his lower lip, evidence that at least part of his dark background was true.

She caught his hand in hers, kissed the palm and held it to her lips as if she never wanted to let it go. "But what about tomorrow?" she whispered as if to herself.

Tomorrow?

Luke heard the soft question with a heavy heart. He'd never promised Arden a tomorrow. He couldn't, not yet. Not when he wasn't sure there was going to be a tomorrow for the two of them together. And not when he was so close to finding the pot of gold at the end of the rainbow.

He glanced back at the chair where he'd left his clothes. The briefcase and its contents were still a temptation. A chance to shed his shaded past and live as he'd never lived before. Until this moment he'd felt he had to take that chance.

Until he made up his mind to deliver the contents

of the briefcase and to return to New York without it, he had to separate Arden from the danger that followed him. A danger that would surely find her if they remained together.

He rested his chin on Arden's gleaming golden curls. The scent of lily of the valley clung to her, along with bittersweet memories of the moments when he'd given her her heart's desire. And filled his own empty heart.

She was a woman who'd found the strength to live her dreams and to find her independence.

He was a man who'd finally found a woman he could love. And love her he did. Too much, and more than she realized.

With a heavy heart, he knew that he loved her enough to have to walk away.

Chapter Thirteen

"I'm afraid we'll have to get a move on if we're going to catch our flight," Luke said reluctantly as he glanced at the large black-and-white clock on the wall. "It's after eight o'clock."

"I wish... I wish last night could go on forever." She tried to smile, but he saw the regret in her eyes.

"Me, too," he said as he lingered for a last kiss. "But that's not the way things work. Life has a terrible way of grinding our noses in reality."

"I prefer dreams."

With a little laugh, he kissed her once, twice, lingering there beside her. He preferred dreams, too, but he knew better than to give in to them. He'd made a promise to himself not to expose her to danger, himself included.

The precious hours of exploring every inch of Arden suddenly didn't seem enough. It was difficult for him to hide his reaction to the creamy white shoulders, soft breasts and hips—hidden but still revealed under the white cotton sheet. A reaction that made him want to gather her in his arms and turn off the world outside the door.

He untangled himself from Arden's arms and lowered his feet to the cold marble floor. "Jeez," he muttered, standing on one foot, "the floor feels like ice."

"Here," Arden said, "take the blanket and put it on the floor. Cancún is bound to be warmer, thank goodness." She wrapped the bedsheet around herself and scrambled after him.

He kept his silence while he turned away to dress. To avoid anyone noticing he'd had his clothes off, he took care to look exactly as he had before, even to the way he knotted his tie.

The time was fast approaching when he would have to say goodbye. Looking back at Arden, he decided there would be time enough for goodbyes after they'd reached Cancún. First, he had to reassure himself she was safely registered at the Majestic Hotel and he could leave her with a clear conscience.

Or could he?

"Luke?"

The question in Arden's voice turned him around just as he was getting ready to snap the damn handcuff around his wrist.

She was poised by the door with her flight bag in her hand. The rumpled I Love NY sweatshirt covered her wedding dress almost to the knee. The long sleeves hung over her hands. He could see the bubble-gum-machine wedding ring on her finger. Traces of mud spattered the white satin shoes which had dried out of shape. Her blond curls were drawn into a ponytail. Even tied back from her face, a few tendrils framed her eyes. She looked as bedraggled as ever.

Still, she managed to look great.

Luke smothered a strangled laugh at the picture she made—a combination of the sugar and spice little girls were made of and a large dose of sensuality. She was all woman and the one with whom he'd shared a few surprisingly passionate early-morning hours.

He didn't dare ask if she was wearing the skimpy bikini.

"You haven't answered me. What do you intend to do when we reach Cancún?"

If she'd asked, he hadn't heard her. He'd been too busy admiring the woman she'd become. And reminding himself of all the reasons he had to let her go.

"I'm not sure," he said evasively, willing himself to return her questioning look without giving away his inner turmoil. He could see from the smiling expression on her face that, after the passion that had passed between them, she believed he would remain in Cancún with her.

He couldn't. For her sake, he had to let her go.

In a crowded resort like Cancún where everyone was a stranger, there were half a dozen ways he could disappear. At one time or another, he'd tried all of them. The disappearance of one tourist wouldn't be noticed.

Her smile slowly faded as he steadfastly returned her gaze. Comprehension slowly dawned on her face. His conscience took a dive as she realized, or at least suspected, he intended to leave her once they'd reached their destination.

"You're not going to stay at Cancún, are you?" she asked quietly. "You're going to leave."

"I have to, I may not have a choice." He cursed

himself for what he was doing to her. He'd hoped to delay the question and the answer until she was safely in Cancún.

Arden's face whitened. She glanced at the rumpled cot where he'd made love to her in what seemed a few heartbeats ago. "Back to New York?"

He shrugged, settled the handcuff around his wrist and snapped it shut with a sharp click. "Maybe. I'm not sure."

She studied him for a minute or two before her gaze focused on the briefcase that dangled from his wrist. "It's because what's in there is more important to you than I am, isn't it?"

Luke glanced sharply at her. How could she have guessed the contents were so vital to him personally? No good could come of her knowing the truth. Especially if she was ultimately questioned about what she knew of him and the contents of the briefcase. He had to skirt the truth, even as he'd told himself there would be no more lies between them.

"Now look, Arden," he said, "I told you before that the less you knew about me the better. I meant it then and I mean it now. And the less you know about the briefcase the better off both of us will be."

"What's in it?" she persisted, never taking her gaze off the briefcase. "You've never answered me when I asked you before. After last night and this morning, you owe me."

He shrugged and busied himself putting his watch on his free right wrist.

"It must be something extremely valuable or it wouldn't be handcuffed to you," she said slowly. A

frown creased her forehead as she studied the briefcase. It was as if she was trying to fit the pieces of a
puzzle together.

He shrugged. "It depends on your definition of
valuable."

"I could understand if the contents were the reason
for all this secrecy. What I can't understand is how
you're able to take the handcuff off whenever you
want to. And especially, why it's so important to
you."

"It just is, Arden. Leave it alone, please!"

A rosy flush covered her face as their eyes met. "If
you can take it off now, why didn't you take it off
when you were making love to me?"

Wounded by Arden's suggestion he had used her,
Luke paused. How could he tell her that from the moment he'd taken her in his arms, he'd been tempted to
remove the handcuff. And that he was sorely tempted
to take it off now. If only to take her back to bed and
show her how much she *had* come to mean to him.
But they had a plane to catch. And he still had to say
goodbye.

"You once told me the people you were going to
deliver the briefcase to were the only ones who had a
key to open the handcuff," she added slowly. "Obviously, that was another lie. Maybe everything from
the time we met has been a lie."

Arden gazed thoughtfully at Luke while he silently
buttoned his overcoat. The truth, when it finally hit
her was almost overwhelming. He couldn't tell her
because he intended to keep the briefcase's contents
for himself!

She'd never felt so empty, so shaken, so cold, as she digested the truth. "You never intended to deliver the briefcase to its rightful owners, did you?"

The look on his face told her she was closer to the truth than he cared for her to be.

"I may have dreamed you up, but I never thought you would turn out to be a criminal like that man Hoyt, or maybe even worse," she told him. "Or that you would take advantage of the trust I put in you."

Luke winced. He started to speak, then helplessly shook his head.

"No, you don't have to answer me if you don't want to. You don't owe me anything. I've been as much to blame as you in all of this, maybe even more. After all, I took you up on your offer to warm me. I'm the one who offered herself to you. Or at least to the man I thought you were. I guess I shouldn't be surprised you took me up on my offer." Her voice broke as she added, "I must have been an easy mark."

"Arden, don't do this to yourself," Luke pleaded. "I swear I never thought of you that way."

"Did you have to tell me you were falling in love with me?" she went on as if he hadn't spoken.

"That part wasn't a lie, Arden," he answered quietly. "Not from the moment you came into my arms last night to keep warm. I didn't realize until later how much I was beginning to care for you."

"Then why are you doing this to us?" She took a hesitant step, reached out to him. "How can you walk away as if nothing happened between us, after all we shared?"

The anguish in her eyes tore at Luke's very soul.

He forced himself to return her stricken gaze without giving his own inner turmoil away. He hadn't been able to tell her the truth about what he'd intended to do before and he couldn't tell her now. Let her think the worst of him, forget him.

"It's better this way," he replied. "More for your sake than mine. Someday you'll realize I'm right."

"I don't believe it has to end like this!" Arden cried. "If you really love me, we can talk things out. If something is wrong, we could make it right, together."

Time was running out, Luke realized as he glanced at his wristwatch. And no matter how hard he tried to distance himself, her distress weakened his resolve to leave. If there was going to be a clear way to end this, it had to be now.

"Look, Arden. I do care for you," he answered. Torn between wanting Arden and trying to protect her, he raked his fingers through his hair. "But a guy like me has to keep moving. I told you before, I'm not the man for you."

A look of acceptance passed over Arden's face. Luke thought how ironic it was that if he was good at anything, it was at hiding the truth.

"Then maybe you'd better leave now," she answered. "I want to be alone for a few minutes." Luke knew she was too proud to ask him to go to Cancún with her or to remain once they were there.

He started to leave, hesitated. "Why don't you come with me? At least until we get on the plane. I'd like to see you safely at the hotel in Cancún."

She shook her head. "I can make it by myself. I

don't want or need anyone to watch over me. Especially not you."

"You're sure?" Luke felt as if she'd stabbed him with a sharp knife. He'd done some things in the past that he'd come to regret, but he was going to regret losing Arden most of all. But he knew he deserved her anger. And more besides.

"I'm sure," she answered, her face averted. "If you're going to leave, do it now!"

"If you won't come with me, at least lock the door behind me," he told her reluctantly. "Don't open it until you're ready to leave. Not even if you hear voices. Not until you know who's out there."

Wordlessly she motioned him away.

"Well, good luck," he said with a last, lingering glance. Arden had changed. She was a strong woman, stronger than she knew. Perhaps even now she was realizing that strength.

She was also the woman who'd taught him he was capable of recognizing and returning true love. Twelve years of dealing with the dark side of life had left him questioning even that part of him. It had been one of the reasons he'd decided to take the contents of the briefcase and disappear. "I hope you find what you're looking for," he told her. "Oh, and Merry Christmas."

He closed the door behind him.

Arden waited until she was alone. Luke McCauley had taught her a hard lesson. Independence didn't come automatically and, if earned, had to be used wisely. One thing was clear: she wasn't going to give her heart away again.

She took a last look around the roomette before she opened the door. The small room might have been designed as a simple, utilitarian rest stop, but for a few hours it had been one step closer to heaven.

"There she is! I told you so!"

"Jane, leave this to me!" a familiar voice thundered. "Arden Crandall, come out of there at once!"

Arden was taken aback to find her father confronting her. He was supposed to be at home preparing his sermon for Christmas services at the church. She was even more surprised to find her mother, her aunt and uncle in a tight group behind him. And hovering dejectedly in the background, with Margo beside him, was John Travers.

"Dad! What are you doing here?"

"And where should I be if not rescuing my only child from the devil's clutches?"

"I don't need rescuing." Arden frowned at her father's choice of words. "And furthermore, Luke's not the devil! I'm fine."

She was surprised to find herself defending Luke after all that had happened. He may not have turned out to be the man she thought he was, but he certainly wasn't evil. As for harming her, he'd only taken what she'd offered and unleashed the sensual woman inside of her in the process.

"That's not what I was led to believe," her father retorted, glowering over her shoulder at the open door of the roomette. "Jane tells me you spent the night with that man who called himself your husband! He told me over the telephone he was going to take care of you. I insist on talking to him."

"He's not here." Arden met his irate gaze with one of her own. The last thing she needed right now was to hear a sermon.

She shot a disgusted look at her aunt.

Her father eyed the rumpled cot visible through the door, the blanket on the floor. "So, he's gone and left you already? Is that how he takes care of you?"

Arden shrugged. When her father used that tone of voice, there was no use trying to talk to him.

Out of the corner of her eye, she could see John wince. Poor man, she thought, he looked as if he'd rather have been anyplace but here. If her father thought bringing him along would change her mind, he should have known better.

Arden's mother moaned and wrung her hands.

Aunt Jane snorted her disbelief.

Margo pushed her way to the head of the group, threw her arms around Arden and drew her aside. "Are you sure you're going to be okay?" she whispered.

"I've never felt better," Arden answered.

"Your aunt told your father all about this guy Luke. You aren't really married to him, are you?"

"No, not really. Luke told that to Dad and Aunt Jane to get them off my case. But we did spend the night together."

"Arden! You didn't!"

"Yes, I did, and it was wonderful" Arden's answer surprised even herself. "And thanks for your notes on THE GREAT AWAKENING. I found I didn't need them after all." She exchanged a secret smile with Margo.

Margo's eyes widened in surprise. "Good girl! I always knew you had it in you." She glanced back at Arden's former fiancé. "Are you thinking of going back to John now that Luke is gone?"

"No," Arden replied. "And no matter what anyone has to say, I am going to take that honeymoon I planned."

"By yourself?"

"Yes."

Margo studied her closely before she asked, "Then you won't mind if I try to console John?"

"He looks as if he could use some consolation at that," Arden answered after a quick glance at the man she'd left waiting at the altar less than twenty-four hours ago. "But are you sure you want to? He's not very…uh, you know…"

"Honey, I've had a crush on the man for years," Margo said with a broad grin. "It was just that once I realized your father had him picked out for you, I wasn't going to do anything to get between you. And as for what he doesn't know about 'you know'…" She paused and glanced over her shoulder thoughtfully. "I'm more than willing to show him how to loosen up and enjoy what he's been missing."

"You're sure?"

"I'm sure," Margo answered with a little grin. "Actually, I like an older man. Who else would put up with someone like me?"

"Arden, that's enough," Arden's father broke in. "Get your things together. We're going home. I have a Christmas sermon to deliver at noon."

"No, I can't go with you," Arden answered with

an ache in her heart for the anguish on his face. But she'd made her decision and she was going to stand her ground.

"You've changed so much you're breaking your mother's and my heart!"

"No, Dad. I never intended to hurt you. But yes, I've changed. I've grown up. Someday you'll be proud of the woman I've become." There was a new life ahead of her with adventures to be tasted. With or without Luke. And no one was going to stop her.

"Arden, come with us now!" her father pleaded.

"Is the storm over?" Arden asked.

"Of course," her father answered crossly, "or we wouldn't be here."

"In that case," Arden answered, "I have a plane to catch."

IT HADN'T BEEN EASY consoling her mother and breaking away from her father. Or saying goodbye to John and Margo and wishing them well. John's face, as Margo patted him on his shoulder and murmured her encouragement, had been one of relief. Not that she blamed him. The past twenty-four hours had probably been more than a staid man like him could take. As for Margo, Arden had no doubts she'd have John ensnared in no time.

And as for the woman she'd called Aunt Jane, as far as she was concerned that relationship was over, too.

She made for the Majestic flight gate.

"Mrs. McCauley, thank goodness you made it here on time! Your husband is already on board. Now come along, we've delayed the flight as long as we could while I was looking for you.''

"My husband?" Arden repeated as the tour leader, Agnes Chambers, fussed over her. "Are you sure?"

"My goodness' sakes, where else did you think the man would be at a time like this? Unless you've had your first argument. But don't let that worry you. It *is* your honeymoon, after all.''

Arden eyed her warily as she remembered the tour documents she had in her purse. What the amiable tour leader didn't know couldn't hurt her. As to what she would say when she saw the name *Travers* on the tickets, after Luke had introduced her as his wife last night, Arden could only guess.

"Now don't you worry," Agnes Chambers reassured, as she urged her along. "Last night was a difficult one for all of us. Although I did hear you were lucky enough to rent a roomette. If your new husband said or did anything to upset you, it was probably just a little misunderstanding due to the stressful situation.''

Misunderstanding? That wasn't what she called it, Arden mused as she followed the woman to the plane's boarding door. Ill-advised, maybe. But, even with the morning's conclusion, spending the hours making love with Luke had been an experience she would never forget. Nor would she forget Luke, either.

In her hurry to board Arden, the tour leader overlooked her documents. Grateful not to have to explain, Arden silently followed her down the plane's single aisle.

"Here you are, Mrs. McCauley," Agnes Chambers

said hurriedly. "We saved you the seat beside your husband. Now, before the storm picks up again, I'll go and tell the captain we're ready. We want to make it out of here this morning while we still can!"

With a sidelong look at Luke, Arden sank into the aisle seat beside him and fastened her seat belt. His head was thrown back, his eyes were closed, but a faint smile hovered on his lips. He may have been pretending to be asleep, but he was very aware of what was going on.

For that matter, asleep or awake, it was going to be difficult to ignore him on the more-than-five-hour plane trip. All she could think of was his smile and the thoughts that must be going through his mind. And what he would do when he "awakened." She stirred restlessly and looked around for an available empty seat.

She heard the engine start and saw the Seat Belt sign light up. It was too late to move or to ask Agnes Chambers for another seat. With the way her luck was going, she would probably have to listen to a lecture from the tour leader on togetherness and how to make a marriage work.

As far as she was concerned, her sixteen-hour "marriage" to Luke had been all the togetherness she could handle. One broken heart was enough.

Luke felt sorry for Arden's obvious discomfiture. If he'd had his druthers, he would have stayed as far away from her as he could get. For her sake, not his. He'd spent the past half hour thinking of the choices confronting him, only to conclude there was no choice at all. Not if he wanted Arden. She was worth more than the contents of the briefcase.

He glanced at her white fingers that tightly grasped the armrest during take off, and grinned. Things weren't as bad as they seemed if she was still wearing the bubble-gum-machine wedding ring.

"Decided to come along with me after all?" he asked.

"Just for the plane ride," she answered coolly, looking down at the briefcase in his lap. "After all, you made yourself very clear." She frowned. "What are you doing here, anyway?"

"I couldn't get a seat on another plane."

"So sit somewhere else."

"No," he answered, reaching for her hand. "I want to be with you."

"Then I'll move!"

"Give it up, Arden," Luke said, holding her hand in his firm grip. "Just give me a few minutes. I want to talk to you."

"Have you changed your plans?"

"Maybe." He smiled as everything fell into place. "Just maybe."

THE SUN BEAT DOWN on the white sands of the private beach in front of the Majestic Hotel. Palm and breadfruit trees swayed in the gentle breeze that came off the water. The sounds of steel drums and tropical music wafted through the air.

Arden sighed happily. "What a great place for a honeymoon!"

Luke murmured his agreement as he turned his full attention to Arden.

"You weren't really going to abscond with whatever was in the briefcase you were carrying, were you?"

"You want me to be honest?"

"Of course."

He turned his face into Arden's bare waist that pillowed his head above the warm, white sand. His lips brushed her sun-drenched, golden skin. His body stirred at the soft gasp she always gave when pleasure became too strong.

"What do you think, love?" he asked as he turned over on his stomach and bent to his task.

"I don't know." She clutched his sable hair and stirred restlessly under his kisses. Her stomach muscles clenched under his searching tongue. "I never can think clearly when you do that."

"Do what?" he teased, feigning innocence. "This?" He reached under her soft middle and brought her beloved body to his lips.

"Yes, that!" she gasped, twining her fingers in his hair. "You have to stop now. We're in plain view of anyone who comes along!"

"This is a honeymoon hotel, sweetheart. And the beach is almost empty. Looks as if everyone went inside for an afternoon siesta." Dark eyes sparkling, Luke winked.

"Luke!" Arden colored at the suggestive tone in his voice and at the sultry expression in his eyes.

"Don't worry, love. If anyone does come along, I'm

sure they'll figure I'm a man doing what a man does on his honeymoon.''

He kissed her through her bikini bra until he heard that tiny gasp he loved to hear. Not satisfied, he buried his head in the hollow of her throat and groaned his frustration.

''Come on, let's go in the water,'' he coaxed. ''At least there's some measure of privacy out there.''

Arden gazed over his head at the still waters. She was tempted, but, by nature, cautious. They'd explored and made love in many unusual places in the past few days, but never out in the open in broad daylight. And certainly not in the clear, warm waters of the Caribbean.

The sun glittered on the unspoiled, calm turquoise waters. An occasional flying fish broke the surface, spun in the air in a graceful arch and plunged back into the water. ''The water's awfully clear,'' she said doubtfully. ''Anyone could see us.''

''I doubt it,'' he replied, and placed a quick kiss on her chin. He picked a loose rose petal out of her hair. ''Most of the other guests have gone off on a tour to the Mayan ruins, anyway. And if someone does pass by, all they'll be able to see is our heads. I'll cover the rest of you,'' he promised with a broad grin that melted the last of her resistance.

Luke had more than delivered on her fantasies on this, their honeymoon. For that matter, he'd even fulfilled a few she hadn't been aware of. She thought dreamily of the rose-petal-strewn bed waiting for her on her wedding night and the hours of passion that had followed.

The more she'd learned about Luke since they'd turned their make-believe marriage into a real one, the more he fascinated her. And, if possible, the more she loved him.

They'd delivered the briefcase to its owners and gone back to New York for their wedding to make her father happy. Her father had married them in a quiet ceremony as soon as they'd obtained a license. At the time, he'd looked perfectly happy to turn her over to Luke's care.

Life with Luke was going to be a mixture of loving, adventure and excitement. She was more than ready for all three. And anything else the future might bring. Especially a son that would look exactly like his father.

Luke lifted her to her feet and took the hand where the phony wedding ring still occupied the place of honor. He'd bought her a real wedding ring, but Arden had insisted she loved the dollar ring too much to replace it.

"Ready?"

"Ready!"

They raced into the warm waters together. By the time they were submerged in shoulder-high water, Luke's laughter had turned into heated glances, his glances to kisses.

The warm, pristine waters closed over Arden's head when Luke playfully pulled her beneath the surface. He released her after a quick kiss and took them to the surface. In moments he wrapped her in his arms and kept his promise. Too well.

"Now, about that siesta," he said when he could catch his breath.

"What's the matter with staying right here?"

Luke shouted with laughter. "You *did* say you were a minister's daughter, didn't you?"

"Yes. But now I'm your wife."

As she lost herself in his arms, Arden fleetingly realized she never did learn what was in the briefcase. Not that it mattered, anyway.

HARLEQUIN®

A M E R I C A N ◆ R O M A N C E®

COMING NEXT MONTH

Next month, celebrate Christmas with American Romance
as we take you
HOME FOR THE HOLIDAYS

#705 CHRISTMAS IN THE COUNTRY by Muriel Jensen
Now that he was free, ex-hostage Jeff James wanted nothing more than to eat Liza deLane's glazed ham for Christmas. But for the woman touted as the "new Martha Stewart," the *timing* couldn't be worse. She had a borrowed husband, rented kids...and a very big problem!

#706 MARLEY AND HER SCROOGE by Emily Dalton
When Carl Merrick fell asleep at his desk on Christmas Eve, his business partner Marley Jacobs made an unexpected appearance in his dreams. Dressed in a baby-doll nightie, she warned him to change his Scroogelike ways by the stroke of midnight or someone else would be sharing her Christmas future.

#707 BELLS, RINGS & ANGELS' WINGS by Linda Randall Wisdom
One minute Libby Barnes idly wished she didn't have to spend Christmas with her family; the next she wished she'd kept her mouth shut. Because there was her house, there were her parents, there was her husband Ty—but nobody knew who *she* was....

#708 THE SANTA SUIT by Karen Toller Whittenburg
Single mom Kate Harmon had always told her twins the truth—Santa Claus didn't exist. So why had they hired detective Gabe Housley to find him? And why was Kate hoping that Gabe was Santa's answer to the twins' request for a daddy?

AVAILABLE THIS MONTH:

#701 IN PAPA BEAR'S BED
Judy Christenberry

#702 A DARK & STORMY NIGHT
Anne Stuart

#703 OVERNIGHT WIFE
Mollie Molay

#704 MISTER CHRISTMAS
Linda Cajio

Look us up on-line at: http://www.romance.net

Every month there's another title from one
of your favorite authors!

October 1997
Romeo in the Rain by Kasey Michaels
When Courtney Blackmun's daughter brought home Mr. Tall,
Dark and Handsome, Courtney wanted to send the young
matchmaker to her room! Of course, that meant the single
New Jersey mom would be left alone with the irresistibly
attractive Adam Richardson....

November 1997
Intrusive Man by Lass Small
Indiana's Hannah Calhoun had enough on her hands taking
care of her young son, and the last thing she needed was a
man complicating things—especially Max Simmons, the
gorgeous cop who had eased himself right into her little boy's
heart…and was making his way into hers.

December 1997
Crazy Like a Fox by Anne Stuart
Moving in with her deceased husband's—*eccentric*—family
in Louisiana meant a whole new life for Margaret Jaffrey and
her nine-year-old daughter. But the beautiful young widow
soon finds herself seduced by the slower pace and the much-
too-attractive cousin-in-law, Peter Andrew Jaffrey....

**BORN IN THE USA: Love, marriage—
and the pursuit of family!**

Available at your favorite retail outlet!

Free Gift Offer

With a Free Gift proof-of-purchase
from any Harlequin® book, you can receive
a beautiful cubic zirconia pendant.

This stunning marquise-shaped stone is a genuine cubic
zirconia—accented by an 18" gold tone necklace.
(Approximate retail value $19.95)

Send for yours today...
compliments of ✦HARLEQUIN®

To receive your free gift, a cubic zirconia pendant, send us one original proof-of-
purchase, photocopies not accepted, from the back of any Harlequin Romance®,
Harlequin Presents®, Harlequin Temptation®, Harlequin Superromance®, Harlequin
Intrigue®, Harlequin American Romance®, or Harlequin Historicals® title available at
your favorite retail outlet, together with the Free Gift Certificate, plus a check or money
order for $1.65 U.S./$2.15 CAN. (do not send cash) to cover postage and handling,
payable to Harlequin Free Gift Offer. We will send you the specified gift. Allow 6 to 8
weeks for delivery. Offer good until December 31, 1997, or while quantities last. Offer
valid in the U.S. and Canada only.

Free Gift Certificate

Name: _____

Address: _____

City: _____ State/Province: _____ Zip/Postal Code: _____

Mail this certificate, one proof-of-purchase and a check or money order for postage
and handling to: HARLEQUIN FREE GIFT OFFER 1997. In the U.S.: 3010 Walden
Avenue, P.O. Box 9071, Buffalo NY 14269-9057. In Canada: P.O. Box 604, Fort Erie,
Ontario L2Z 5X3.

FREE GIFT OFFER   084-KEZ
ONE PROOF-OF-PURCHASE
To collect your fabulous FREE GIFT, a cubic zirconia pendant, you must include this
original proof-of-purchase for each gift with the properly completed Free Gift Certificate.

084-KEZR

HARLEQUIN WOMEN KNOW ROMANCE WHEN THEY SEE IT.

And they'll see it on **ROMANCE CLASSICS**, the new 24-hour TV channel devoted to romantic movies and original programs like the special *Romantically Speaking—Harlequin™ Goes Prime Time.*

Romantically Speaking—Harlequin™ Goes Prime Time introduces you to many of your favorite romance authors in a program developed exclusively for Harlequin® readers.

Watch for *Romantically Speaking—Harlequin™ Goes Prime Time* beginning in the summer of 1997.

If you're not receiving ROMANCE CLASSICS, call your local cable operator or satellite provider and ask for it today!

Escape to the network of your dreams.

See Ingrid Bergman and Gregory Peck in *Spellbound* on Romance Classics.

FREE BOOK OFFER!

With every Harlequin Ultimate Guides™ order, receive a FREE bonus book!

#80507	HOW TO TALK TO A NAKED MAN	$4.99 U.S. ☐	$5.50 CAN. ☐
#80508	I CAN FIX THAT	$5.99 U.S. ☐	$6.99 CAN. ☐
#80510	WHAT YOUR TRAVEL AGENT KNOWS THAT YOU DON'T	$5.99 U.S. ☐	$6.99 CAN. ☐
#80511	RISING TO THE OCCASION More Than Manners: Real Life Etiquette for Today's Woman	$5.99 U.S. ☐	$6.99 CAN. ☐
#80513	WHAT GREAT CHEFS KNOW THAT YOU DON'T	$5.99 U.S. ☐	$6.99 CAN. ☐
#80514	WHAT SAVVY INVESTORS KNOW THAT YOU DON'T	$5.99 U.S. ☐	$6.99 CAN. ☐

(quantities may be limited on some titles)

TOTAL AMOUNT	$
POSTAGE & HANDLING	$
($1.00 for one book, 50¢ for each additional)	
APPLICABLE TAXES*	$ _____
TOTAL PAYABLE	$ _____
(check or money order—please do not send cash)	

*New York residents remit applicable sales taxes.
Canadian residents remit applicable GST and provincial taxes.

To order, complete this form and send it, along with a check or money order for the total above, payable to Harlequin Ultimate Guides, to: **In the U.S.:** 3010 Walden Avenue, P.O. Box 9047, Buffalo, NY 14269-9047; **In Canada:** P.O. Box 613, Fort Erie, Ontario, L2A 5X3.

Look us up on-line at: http://www.romance.net   NFPOP